# JOSIE AND THE PUSSYCATS™

**Written by Cathy East Dubowski and Jackie Jarosz
Based on a motion picture screenplay
written by Deborah Kaplan & Harry Elfont
Based on characters appearing in Archie Comics.
The Josie and the Pussycats characters were created
for Archie Comics by Richard H. Goldwater
and Dan DeCarlo with John L. Goldwater.**

HarperEntertainment
*An Imprint of HarperCollinsPublishers*

HARPERENTERTAINMENT
*An Imprint of* HarperCollins*Publishers*
10 East 53rd Street
New York, NY 10022-5299

**Parents please consult movie rating at www.filmratings.com <http://www.filmratings.com> when making viewing choices for your children.**

HarperCollins books are available at special quantity discounts for bulk purchases for sales promotions, premiums, or fund-raising. For information please call or write: Special Markets Department, HarperCollins Publishers Inc., 10 East 53rd Street, New York, New York 10022-5299. Telephone: (212) 207-7528. Fax: (212) 207-7222.

ISBN: 0-06-103201-8

HarperCollins ®, 🏛 ®, and HarperEntertainment™ are trademarks of HarperCollins Publishers Inc.

Text and photo insert designed by Elizabeth M. Glover.

First Printing: April 2001

Printed in the United States of America

Visit HarperEntertainment on the World Wide Web at
www.harpercollins.com

Visit Josie and the Pussycats at www.archiecomics.com

10  9  8  7  6  5  4  3  2  1

# JOSIE AND THE PUSSYCATS™

# 1

"I can't believe it!" the girl said breathlessly into the television reporter's microphone. "I mean, like I can't believe that I'm actually going to get to see them in the flesh because"— tears began to stream down her face, making tiny gray rivulets of mascara down her cheeks—"like, Du Jour is like, my favorite band of all time!"

All around her other girls screamed their agreement. In fact, the airport was mobbed with thousands of teenagers who'd come here for one reason: to see the hottest boy band of all time in person. Rumor had it that they'd be showing up any minute in a limo to catch their plane to their next concert.

Music blared from dozens of boom boxes, playing Du Jour's latest CD. Everyone in the crowd knew every word, every harmony, and sang along with an almost religious fervor.

And it wasn't just girls who were insane for the band. The reporter squeezed through the crowd and held the mike up to a very emotional thirteen-year-old boy. "They rock!" he shouted. "I've got all their CDs and all their trading cards and all my gear is from their clothing line—Du Jour Couture. Man, I straight up love them!" He paused and his eyes shifted nervously. "You know—like brothers."

Another girl in the crowd fell to her knees crying hysterically. "I . . . I just want to touch them. I don't care which one. I don't care where!"

Suddenly a deafening roar rose above the already ear-shattering screams. This was bigger than Elvis, bigger than Beatlemania—bigger than all the other boy bands combined.

The crying fan looked around, desperately searching the area like a combat soldier ready for attack. "Oh, my god they're here!" she shrieked. "THEY'RE HERE!"

Then the crowd of screaming teenagers seemed to turn into one living collective body, focusing its entire life-force on a single object: a Hummer limo driving past the security barriers onto the tarmac, blasting the new Du Jour single over built-in speakers. It rolled to a stop in front of a private jet bearing the Du Jour logo.

The crowd went berserk. They screamed, waved, and held up homemade banners that said, "DU JOUR RULES" and "WE LOVE YOU 4 EVER!" The crowd began to chant: "We want Du Jour! We want Du Jour!"

And then, as if choreographed for one of Du Jour's slick dance routines, four doors of the limo opened at exactly the same moment, and the boys of Du Jour stepped out.

There was Marco, the sexy Latino boyfriend who set girls' hearts on fire.

DJ DJ, whose dark eyes and hip-hop dance moves turned fans to Jell-O.

Travis, the unshaved rebel grown women secretly dreamed of running away with.

And Les, the blond boy-next-door type whom every daughter—and mother—in the country wished really lived next door.

*Something for everybody.* The girls adored them. The boys adored them and wanted to be them. And stores could barely keep their CDs, clothes, action figures, and sports bottles in stock.

Without missing a beat, the lads of Du Jour fell into line and began dancing steps they could do in their sleep—and probably did—

lip-synching to the music, taking turns for a front-and-center solo moment before returning to their place in line. It was like something straight out of a music video. And a lot like a beauty pageant.

Whatever, the crowd loved it, and the screaming grew louder and louder—especially when the guys finished and started walking toward the security barriers. And when they actually began touching outstretched hands and signing autographs, girls fainted. Boys cried.

Meanwhile, totally unnoticed by Du Jour's adoring fans, tall handsome Wyatt Frame stepped out of Du Jour's limo and checked his reflection in the tinted window. Thirty-something and incredibly well-dressed, he was one of the most powerful men in the world right now—because he was in charge of Du Jour.

He watched the well-orchestrated media event for a moment, allowing the fans just enough—but not too much—time to interact with the band. He scanned the crowd, making a mental note of how many TV news crews had shown up for a sound bite. After a few more carefully choreographed seconds, he checked his watch, then calmly walked over to the crowd. "Come on, boys," he told Du Jour in his upper-class English accent. "We don't want to be late."

The kids at the front of the crowd screamed "Nooo!" but the world's most famous boys instantly turned and fell back into formation, dancing their way to their private jet, dancing up the stairs, blowing kisses as they disappeared into the plane.

Wyatt followed them, but turned at the top of the steps and looked out at the sea of screaming teens. He smiled for a moment, just reveling in the mania he'd helped to create . . . even imagining for one tiny moment that all those hysterical teenagers were screaming for him. *Wy-att, Wy-att, Wy-att . . .*

Then he shook the fantasy from his mind and ducked inside. He was a grown man now, and grown men had a lot more fun than teenage boys. Especially when they ruled the boys who ruled.

Soon the private jet was streaking across the sky toward the next scheduled stop on the Du Jour tour. Wyatt leaned back in his seat and closed his eyes for a rare moment of rest and relaxation. Baby-sitting a bunch of teenage boys who thought they were hot stuff wasn't the easiest job in the world. But things were going smoothly so far.

At last the pilot turned off the FASTEN SEATBELT signs, and Wyatt got up to talk to the guys. They were already partying, drinking champagne, snacking on hors d'oeuvres catered by the finest local restaurants—enjoying the good life.

Wyatt cringed as he watched Marco feeding obscenely expensive gourmet hors d'oeuvres to that ridiculous pet monkey of his. But Wyatt was on strict orders to indulge the boys their little whims, so he held his tongue.

"Okay," Wyatt said, going over the itinerary. "We land at Riverdale in half an hour. We do the song and dance at the airport, then over to the—" He paused to check a card. "*Riverdale Rise and Shine* show. Then an afternoon in-store prior to sound check, then concert at eight." He looked up at the boys, who looked totally bored. "Questions?"

"Yo, Wyatt," Marco said. "Why's my limited-edition Coke can have me with a goatee? Everybody knows I shaved it into a soul patch for our 'Don't Tell Your Poppa' video. This is whack." He put his monkey down and held up the offensive can.

Before Wyatt could answer, DJ interrupted. "No, what's really whack is that dirty monkey." He held up his designer duffel. "Damn monkey pooed all up in my bag!"

Marco shrugged. "You don't give Dr. Zeus the love, he gives you the poo."

"Gentlemen, gentlemen!" Wyatt intervened,

holding up his hands. "We'll talk to Coke about the cans. And Marco please try and clean up after the Doctor."

Wyatt made a note in his Palm VII, then looked around.

"By the way," Travis grumbled.

Wyatt groaned inwardly and sighed. "Yes, Travis?"

"I thought *I* was the only one who was supposed to have Pure Platinum tips. Marco was supposed to have Honey whatever, but now his look just like mine."

Wyatt rubbed his temples. He felt a honey of a headache coming on.

"What," Marco snapped. "You like, *own* Pure Platinum? You're like, the Pure Platinum *owner*?" He shoved his face up in Travis's mug, a challenge blazing in his eyes.

Travis's fists shot up.

The monkey began to screech—

"Boys!" Wyatt cried, stepping in between them. He took a deep breath, then slowly let it out. This was the kind of stupid quibbling that landed stars on the front pages of those grocery store gossip rags. Not the kind of publicity Wyatt's boss wanted to see. If it were up to Wyatt, he'd love nothing more than to give these bratty boys what they really deserved—a good old-fashioned spanking for misbehaving.

7

But it wasn't up to him. His job was to be the diplomat, the public relations man . . . *The nanny*, he thought miserably.

"Look," he told the boys, slipping a calming hand on Marco and Travis's shoulders. "This is obviously the fault of the hair team. No reason to explode, hmm?"

Travis relaxed a bit and took a half step back. Marco lowered his fists. But both still glared at each other like opposing generals in a small war.

"I'll get it all ironed out when we land," Wyatt promised in his most soothing voice.

Snarling, Travis flopped back down in his seat and propped his feet up on the seat in front of him.

Marco turned away, stroking his monkey.

Wyatt straightened his jacket and made a new note in his Palm Pilot, then looked up with an exaggerated smile. "How are we now? Good? Happy?"

A couple of shrugs were all the answer he got.

*Rude brats*, Wyatt thought bitterly. Then turned to his own seat.

"Actually, Wyatt . . ."

Wyatt froze, his back to the boys, and rolled his eyes heavenward, though he was definitely not a praying man. With great effort he smiled and turned around. "Ye-e-e-s?" he asked, like the concierge at a four-star hotel, eager to indulge his guest's every whim.

Les stood there a moment, his face twisted in the same forlorn frown he'd worn on the last album cover. *The confused cow look*, Wyatt secretly called it.

"There is one more thing," Les said.

Wyatt did a quick draw with his Palm Pilot again, ready to make his usual grand show of making a note of it. Sometimes "making a note of it" was *all* he did about one of the boys' complaints, but it seemed to make them feel secure to have Wyatt *act* as if he gave a damn.

*What is it this time?* Wyatt longed to say out loud. *Not enough Mountain Dew in the hospitality fridge? Forgot the videotapes of your favorite cartoon? Need a night-light? Your teddy bear? A binky?*

"We were working on a remix of the last single when we found this weird background track," Les said. He almost scratched his head, then stopped, as if realizing he might mess up his heavily gelled hair. "I was wondering if you could explain. . . ."

Wyatt's expression didn't change. But inside all his vital signs went on Red Alert. Selfish petty demands were one thing. He could easily take care of those. But explanations—especially dealing with Du Jour's recorded music—were another matter altogether.

Les handed Wyatt a tape player, and Wyatt slipped on the headphones, carefully schooling his expression so as not to reveal anything he was thinking. He listened for a few moments, feigning a puzzled look, then suddenly his face seemed to turn to stone. He tore off the headphones, snapped open the player, and—like a magician doing a sleight-of-hand card trick—quickly palmed the tape and slipped it into his coat pocket.

Then he snapped the tape player closed and looked up at the boys, his face as innocent as an angel's. "Gee. You know? I have *no* idea what that was."

"Then who put it on there?" DJ challenged.

"We want some answers," Travis demanded.

Wyatt's smile tightened. "Then answers I will provide," he said reassuringly, like a waiter who'd been told a diner's order wasn't quite right. He leaned forward and in a hushed voice, with just the merest hint of a wink, he added, "I'll be right back."

Then he turned on his heel and headed into the cockpit. The door whooshed closed.

DJ leaned back in his plush seat and smiled. "Wyatt's the man."

The boys of Du Jour all nodded their agreement, then sat back and relaxed. Wyatt was not a bad dude, for a toady, they thought. And he was devoted to Du Jour.

They were confident he would take care of everything.

*So the little boys just had to go and get too big for their britches, didn't they?* Wyatt muttered under his breath as he strode down the narrow passage to the airplane's cockpit. *Couldn't be satisfied with being undeservedly and outrageously rich and famous, with practically every nubile young girl dying to throw herself at their feet, could they? Had to start asking questions. . . . Sticking their silly pierced noses into places where they didn't belong. . . . messing up a good thing.*

*Well, their mamas should have warned them— when little boys play with the big boys, guess who gets hurt?*

*And I,* Wyatt thought with a sigh, *get to clean up the mess. . . .*

Wyatt slipped into the cockpit and quietly, but firmly, shut the door. The pilot didn't even glance up as Wyatt leaned over the man's shoulder and said in a deep, quiet voice, "Take the Chevy to the Levee."

The pilot nodded slightly. Without a word, he made a few adjustments on the control panel, stood up and tossed his pilot's cap into the empty seat, then strapped a parachute onto his back.

Wyatt put one on, too.

Moments later the pilot tugged open the emergency exit and, without a backward glance, jumped out.

For a moment Wyatt stood clutching the edges of the metal door, enjoying the feel of the wind as it whipped around his face. *The winds of change*, he chuckled as he peered down through the wisps of angelic white clouds to the patchwork fields below. *Where are we?* he wondered. He had no idea. But it didn't matter. Wherever he was, he knew that at that very moment there were thousands of kids listening to the music of Du Jour. Thousands waiting to pay any price to see their idols live in concert. Thousands of beautiful young girls dreaming of spending the night in any of the boys' arms.

Wyatt laughed and shook his head. What he wouldn't give to be in one of those idiot boys' shoes.

Or rather, he would have traded places with them this morning. Not now.

*Fools!* he thought. *This time you really screwed up.*

Wyatt let go of the doors. *It's been fun, guys— not!* And without a glance back, he jumped.

Back in the plane, Travis posed before a large mirror, scrutinizing his gym-toned abs. Checking out his cool trend-setting clothes. Admiring his Pure Platinum tips, confident that his main man Wyatt would soon fix things so that only he would wear this audacious look . . . when something odd outside the window of the plane caught his eye. "Huh?" He stepped over to the window and leaned down for a better look. "Hey! Check it out!" he called to the others. "See that guy out there with the parachute? Man, he looks just like Wyatt!"

The boys of Du Jour, who had grown up taking dirty, crowded subways to their endless auditions, were so spoiled now that they often got bored even on these luxury flights, and so they quickly crowded over for something interesting to look at.

But as Marco leaned over to get a closer peek, Travis glanced back and saw those Pure Platinum tips sticking up in his face. *Damn, but they look better on me!* Travis thought selfishly. No way was he going to be the one to switch to Honey *anything! I was Pure Platinum first!* he thought. *And it's mine till I give it up.* He grinned. *Maybe I'll just pull them out of Marco's head!* He grabbed hold of Marco's hair with both fists, igniting the fight that had been brewing since the flight began.

DJ and Les were easily distracted by the action. Hey, hair's a major thing to a teen idol.

And as the boys brawled like third graders in the schoolyard, the guy in the parachute who looked like Wyatt was instantly and completely forgotten. . . .

Meanwhile Wyatt floated gracefully toward the earth. How peaceful and quiet it all seemed to him, compared to the infantile squabbling and monkey shrieking he'd left behind on the plane. Up ahead he could see what looked like some small all-American town. . . . No towering skyscrapers blocked the sun from shining on the happy people he imagined must live there, no eight-lane traffic jams tangled and twisted around its city limits, no dark cloud of pollution hovered over it, revealing an aura of sin and doom. An old-fashioned kind of town. *Like something out of an old black-and-white movie,* he thought. Or the comic books he used to read as a kid.

But he'd bet his cell phone that the hick kids who lived there were still maniacally obsessed with every sound that fell from the golden lips of the boys of Du Jour.

*Poor kiddies,* Wyatt thought sarcastically. *They're in for some absolutely heart-breaking news. . . .*

And before Wyatt's expensive Italian shoes even touched the ground, he had whipped out his ubiquitous cell phone and placed a call.

A woman answered the phone. *"What?"*

Wyatt swallowed past the nervous lump in his throat, then delivered the news. "Looks like we need to find another band."

He held the phone away from his ear as the woman bellowed her response. No sense exposing himself to the risk of brain cancer when he didn't have to, he rationalized.

Behind him, far off in the beautiful blue sky, Du Jour's plane appeared as tiny and fragile as a toy as it tilted and dipped among the clouds, then sliced toward the ground, faster and faster, until it sputtered out of sight along the horizon.

As Wyatt's feet finally touched the ground, he jogged a few steps to slow down, then quickly escaped from the parachute twisting in the breeze as easily as he'd escaped the crisis brewing in the sky.

A loud *BOOM!* shook the ground, and Wyatt instinctively reached out for something to hold on to. When Wyatt caught his breath again, he realized he'd landed next to a sign by the side of a two-lane road leading into town. He stepped back and read the plain upright letters:

WELCOME TO RIVERDALE

"Ri-ver-dale . . ." he said slowly, auditioning the sound. *What a corny name for a town.* But then he smiled. America loved nothing better than small-town nobodies who made it big. *Riverdale* would look marvelous on the bio of the next teen music sensation to sweep the nation.

Grinning at his luck, Wyatt flipped open his cell phone again to call directory assistance. Would they even have a taxi service in this Podunk town? he wondered as he waited impatiently through three rings. He hoped so. He needed to get into town fast. He had places to go, people to see.

Before the day was over, he had to discover—i.e., scrounge up—the *new* Du Jour.

# 2

Music exploded through the small club—loud and raw and totally untamed. Josie McCoy, lead singer of the Pussycats, wailed out the words that came straight from her heart. Her fingers seemed to dance their own magic on the well-worn electric guitar as she completely lost herself in the song—in thoughts and feelings that she could only seem to truly express through music.

There was nowhere else in the world she'd rather be than here, nothing she'd rather be doing than making music. With all her heart and soul she knew, this was what she was born to do.

Tall, foxy Valerie Brown grooved away on the bass beside her, instinctively blending her sounds with Josie's in a way that only a best friend could. Drop-dead blond Melody Valentine pounded her drums as she drove the trio toward its climax—and then the song ended.

Josie kept her eyes closed to savor the moment as the last quiver of sound vibrated off into the universe.

The audience was silent, hushed, almost reverent—just the way Josie always felt when everything came together like magic and the music rocked.

And then a strange sound grew in the silence, like a bowling ball rolling down a wooden floor, crescendoing into a sound like a bowling bowl smashing into pins—

Josie leaned into the mike, breathless, sweat glistening on her skin, and said, "Thank you."

The crowd cheered like it was the last few seconds of the Super Bowl. Josie beamed, relishing the sound, then slowly opened her eyes as if waking from a dream. . . .

And came back to reality with a thud.

The "club" the Pussycats were performing their latest gig at was actually the slightly seedy Riverdale Bowling Alley. The farthest lane against the wall had been roped off for their stage, and the lights and acoustics were terrible.

Now Josie realized that the customers weren't even listening to her music—much less applauding it. The cheering came from a group of middle-aged guys celebrating a teammate's spare over on lane 2.

Josie winced and ran a frustrated hand through her red hair. *Don't sweat it,* she scolded herself for the millionth time. All the great bands started off playing in low-rent dives. All the great musicians—from jazz and blues to rock and roll—made music because they *had* to, for the buzz it gave them, not for the money or the applause. All the tough times you had to go through—paying your dues—was the compost, she always told Valerie and Melody. Those times were the fertilizer that made the music rich—what made it grow.

That's what she felt was missing sometimes in those instant boy bands who were hand-picked by producers trying to create a product to sell. Some of that music was so overproduced, synthesized, and sanitized that Josie never knew for sure if it was a real person she heard singing, or a computer.

Josie liked music raw and real and un-slick—the kind you could tell was being made by real human beings. The kind you knew would sound the same live in your own living room as on MTV.

She glanced at her bandmates and her shoulders sagged. Valerie and Melody looked as bummed as she felt.

But Josie was a trooper. She leaned into the mike and said, "Thanks. Thanks for coming out. You're a . . ." What could she say? *You're all a bunch of rude, insensitive jerks who wouldn't recognize good music if a jukebox full of Johnny Cash singles fell on you?* "You're . . . a great crowd," she choked out.

"Any requests?" Valerie tried, hoping for a little interaction with the crowd.

A guy with a revolting beer belly held up two bowling balls and made a rude suggestion as to what she could do with them.

Valerie didn't hesitate a quarter note beat— she hauled off and punched the guy. He dropped like a stone.

And just about as quick, the girls were thrown out on the curb.

Josie winced as a bowling alley employee tossed their last piece of equipment out the door. "Hey! Be careful with that!" she shouted.

The guy grunted and slammed the door.

Josie sighed. Kicked out of a bowling alley! *Man, this gig must really be adding character to our music,* she thought grimly.

"So," said Melody—sweet, ever-cheerful Melody, who loved puppies and kittens and rainbows and sprinkles—"how'd we do?"

Josie pulled a few bills out of her pants

pocket. "Well, minus the ten bucks for that guy's ice pack . . ." She shot Valerie a look.

"Sorry," Val muttered. At least she was remorseful.

Josie counted the bills. "We made three dollars," she announced proudly. With a grand flourish, she handed each girl one single dollar bill.

"Hey, at least we're getting out of the garage," Josie said philosophically. "I mean, all things considered, it was probably our best show."

"Definitely," Melody agreed cheerfully. She neatly folded her bill and deposited it in her pocket. She could see the bright side to a flat tire.

Val inspected her pay, her face as dour as the engraving of George Washington that adorned it. "I love being a rock star," she said dryly.

Suddenly a trendy new sports utility vehicle screeched to a halt at the curb mere inches from the Pussycats' gear. The front window slid open, releasing high-pitched catty laughter and a cloud of perfume.

"Ewww," Josie muttered. She had no idea they could pack that many highlighted, implanted, underdressed Barbie dolls into a single SUV.

"Look!" one of the girls squealed from the

car as she pointed out the window. "Skanky had a rock show and nobody came!"

Her friends burst into hysterical giggles.

Valerie lunged toward the car, but Melody managed to hold her back before she could inflict Pussycat scratches on any of the overly made-up nose-jobbed faces. "Count to ten, Val," she warned her. *"Breathe."*

Val had a chili-hot temper even on the coldest winter day. Josie and Melody had finally chipped in and bought her a book called *12 Steps to Anger Management.* So far it didn't seem to be helping much.

Valerie struggled against Melody's arms a moment more, then with a great deal of effort backed off. But her glare would have peeled paint off the car if she'd been any closer.

"So," Josie said to the girls. "Did you guys all coordinate before leaving the house, or are you just wearing the exact same clothes by accident?"

"At least we're not wearing stupid *bunny* ears!" a girl in the backseat shrieked.

Now even Melody was getting angry. "They're not bunny!" she shot back indignantly. "They're leopard. And they're not stupid, they're *special*. We're special!"

"Yeah," the first girl in the car screamed. *"Blue plate* special!"

This brought even bigger laughs from the other girls. I wonder if *Saturday Night Live* has any openings, Josie thought, wanly.

"I'm sure *Du Jour* will think we look great. . . ." the girl in the backseat went on. She waved a handful of tickets in the girls' faces.

"Front row!" the girl beside her bragged.

"I'm *so* jealous," Valerie said sarcastically. "Like we'd wanna see Du Jour."

"Well, you should," the first girl shot back. "Maybe it'd help you losers learn how a real band busts some moves."

Josie stared at the girl in amazement. "You just said 'bust some moves'!" She couldn't help it—she burst out laughing, and Valerie and Melody joined her.

The first girl scowled. "Laugh it up, you no-talent losers." When that didn't get a rise out of them, she glanced pointedly at the bowling alley behind them and added, "Enjoy the gutters, Josie—because you'll be playing there forever!"

As the driver screeched off in her shiny new car, an empty Diet Coke flew out the back window and bounced off the side of the Pussycats' van. Josie couldn't tell if it made a dent—the van was so old and beat up—but she couldn't stop it from putting a small dent in her big dreams.

With a scowl, Josie yanked open the back doors of the van and began to load up their gear. Valerie and Melody were silent as they helped put instruments and equipment inside.

*What if she's right?* Josie couldn't help but wonder. *What if the Pussycats are no-talent losers?*

She locked up the back, then headed around to the driver's side of her van. *We just need to get out of here,* she told herself firmly. Get something to eat. . . . She and her friends had elected *not* to sample the dubious cuisine they were selling inside the bowling alley. But as she jerked open her door, she glanced back at the place. The Riverdale Bowling Alley must have looked nice and new once—like maybe in the fifties? But now the place was just old and rundown—not in a cool, funky sort of way, but as if nobody really cared about it anymore. A few guys stumbled out carrying their bowling ball bags, laughing and staggering under the influence of a few two many beers, celebrating their win like it was some major event in the history of humanity. One of the guys crammed the last of a hot dog into his mouth and tossed the trash on the already littered sidewalk.

*What a dump.* Josie jumped in the van and turned her keys in the ignition, growling when she had to pump the gas a couple times to get the old engine to start. At last she was able to pull away.

But would she ever really be able to leave places like the bowling alley behind?

*Am I just kidding myself? Is this where I'll be playing forever?*

# 3

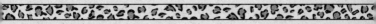

Josie drove for home. They'd all feel better once they got back in their own digs, she told herself.

Josie, Valerie, and Melody shared a house in one of Riverdale's nicest, newest neighborhoods.

Sort of.

To reach their house, Josie had to drive down a lovely street past grand homes with beautiful landscaping, the kind of homes many people dream of owning.

*McMansions*, Josie called them. They all looked alike, with their showy facades and matching mailboxes and identical SUVs parked in the spotless driveways.

The Pussycats' house was at the end of the road, a bit past the huge homes, down a gravel drive, actually, that had been there long before the new subdivision had even been imagined. They had to pass an overgrown field to get to their house—a dilapidated ranch built in the 1960s that their neighbors tried to forget existed. Cats prowled in and out of the lawn statues and flea market junk that filled the yard. They even had an antique in the backyard—a clothesline, where they sometimes actually hung out their wash to dry in the sun.

The place was small, with only one tiny bathroom, but it was all theirs, and they loved it.

Josie parked the van and got her guitar out of the back. While Valerie and Melody went to try to dig up something to eat, Josie headed for her bedroom. On the drive home she'd begun to deal with her feelings the way she usually did . . . by listening to them swirl and simmer in her brain until the idea for a new song began to form.

Soon she was letting it all out through the magic of electricity singing through her guitar. As the new song began to take shape, she caught sight of herself in the mirror.

She ran a hand through her hair, checked out her face—the big eyes and round face could look too cute sometimes, too sweet. Maybe it wasn't their music that was holding them back, she thought. Maybe it was their look. As she played, louder and harder, she began to pose for the mirror, curling her lip like Joan Jett, pretending she was on stage. She had to be sexier, wilder—more outlandish.

*"Nice moves!"* she heard someone shout through the music.

Startled, Josie spun around. "Alan M.!" she exclaimed as the neck of her guitar hit a lamp, sending it crashing to the floor. Totally embarrassed, she ignored the lamp, even though the cord was now dangling from the guitar. She smoothed her hair and said casually, "What's going on?"

Alan M., Josie's best guy friend, and the main subject of many of her most secret fantasies, shrugged his broad shoulders. "The truck's dead."

"Dude . . ." Josie rolled her eyes. Alan M. was a total babe, and a struggling folksinger whose music could make her swoon, but the dude was a dud when it came to the most basic car maintenance problems. "Ever think maybe you should've taken auto shop with me instead of pottery?" she asked as she untangled herself from her guitar . . . and the lamp.

Alan M. threw up his hands in a mock gesture of helplessness as he led the way out of her room. "But all the hot girls took pottery."

Josie glanced back at her perky face in the

mirror before following him out. "All the hot girls . . ." she said with a sigh.

Outside, as Josie worked under the hood of his beat-up truck, Alan M. picked up his acoustic guitar and began to sing. "Did I bust the carburetor? Overload the alternator?"

Josie laughed and sang along, "Abused the accelerator . . . ?"

Alan M. smiled back at her, and her heart began to pound like hip hop cranked up loud on a car radio. What she wouldn't do for a chance to duet with him for real. And she knew they'd be good together—she'd seen and heard them together hundreds of times in her dreams.

Dreams that had to remain dreams, she reminded herself, as long as Alan M. just saw her as a pal.

"You don't have to stomp on it," she said a little harsher than she meant to as she stood up and wiped her hands on a rag. "You know, Alan M., you don't deserve a truck this good. You totally take it for granted."

*Are we talking about the truck here, Josie?* asked a little voice inside her head. *Or your heart?*

"The truck," Josie repeated emphatically.

Alan M. grinned and strummed his guitar. "Takin' my truck for granted, she says I'm taking my truck for granted. . . ."

Josie ducked back under the hood, afraid her cheeks were flaming.

And then Alan M. stopped suddenly and leaned his elbows on his guitar. "Hey, Jose . . . did'ya ever wanna tell someone something, but you just . . . you just weren't sure if you should?"

Josie gulped and just barely missed bashing her head on the hood of the truck as she looked up hopefully. "Uh . . . yeah."

Alan M. laid his instrument aside and joined her under the hood. His voice grew hushed and intimate. "I mean, 'cause like you just weren't sure how they'd react or if it was really . . . the right thing to do?"

Josie stared into his eyes, her face inches from his face, her lips a breathless kiss away from his lips. . . . When she could speak again, she breathed, "It's *always* the right thing to do. Telling someone. Always tell. Always." Her eyes began to flutter closed, her face turned up to his . . .

" 'Cause there's this guy at work, and he just reeks, you know?"

Josie froze. Her eyes blinked a few times as she tried to process the totally unexpected information. "A guy. A smelly guy."

"No, I mean *really* smelly," Alan M. explained. "Like, like—man, I can't even describe it. I mean, you'd say something, right? No one else seems to want to, but really, it's just . . . well, it's just wrong. You know? He smells like a stadium bathroom."

Josie tried to stuff her feelings back down into the vault she called her heart. "Yeah," she said gruffly. "You should definitely say something." She turned back to the truck and tried to keep the tears from welling up in her eyes.

"I love that I can talk to you about stuff, you know?" Alan M. said, totally oblivious. "It's really cool."

"That's what I'm here for." Josie slammed the hood shut a little harder than was necessary. "You're all set."

Alan M. jumped in his truck. It cranked up on the first try. He leaned out the window, beaming at her with a smile that could melt the hardest heart. "You rule, Jose! I'll call you later."

Josie watched him drive away, totally bummed.

If only she could fix broken hearts as easily as she did cars.

Inside Josie found her roommates serving a bowl of steaming hot ramen noodles. One bowl. For all of them.

JOSIE AND THE PUSSYCATS

Rock stars had to eat cheap when they only made three dollars a gig.

The Pussycats had a system. Each girl would carefully take a forkful of noodles, then pass the bowl to the right. Then she'd squeeze a few drips from a little packet of soy sauce onto the noodles, then pass that to the right. If there was any left at the end, the bowl got passed around for a second helping.

"Mmm, good ramen," Josie lied.

The girls chewed slowly, ceremoniously.

*Pathetic*, Josie thought with a sigh.

"Who would have thought one pack could go so far," Valerie said. She turned another page in her *12 Steps to Anger Management*.

Melody closed her eyes and swallowed. "I wonder if this is what Japan tastes like?"

"What died in here?" The girls' luncheon was suddenly interrupted by an uninvited guest. Alexandra Cabot, spoiled-rotten only daughter of one of Riverdale's richest families, strode into the humble room like a supermodel walking down the runway at a major fashion show. It was a pretty tough feat in a kitchen this small, but Alexandra pulled it off. She paused directly in front of the girls to check her freshly manicured nails, and give the Pussycats a chance to admire her designer ensemble and perfectly styled skunk-streaked black hair.

"Oh, must be your pathetic little hopes and dreams." She looked around and fanned the air in front of her nose. "Well, someone at least crack a window."

"Only if I can shove you out of it," Valerie said, slamming her anger management book closed.

"What are you doing here?" Josie asked.

"Daddy says Cabots have to devote one day a week to charity," Alexandra replied. She dug into the pocket of her Gucci jeans and tossed a penny on the table. "Finished!"

Valerie shot out of her chair, but Melody pulled her back down. "Val!"

Tightly gripping her anger book, Valerie sat back down, chanting under her breath: " 'Good people don't get angry. . . . Good people don't get angry.' "

"See?" Melody said brightly. "We can all be friends." She turned and gave their visitor a bright cheerful smile. "Hi, Alexandra! How are you?"

"Bite me, Bambi."

Alexandra's brother Alexander—trendy casual clothes, tinted aviators, long sideburns—strode in just in time to stop the brawl. He dangled a bag of Krispy Kremes in front of the Pussycats. "Who brought doughnuts?" he sang.

"Wow," Josie said sarcastically. "Cabot charity knows no bounds."

"Hey, I'll take 'em," Valerie said, grabbing for the bag. She and Melody immediately dug into the doughnuts. "Thank goodness we saved room for dessert," Val quipped.

Alexandra shook her head in disbelief. "Good management skills, brother," she drawled. "Build yourself a nice fat girl group." She looked Josie up and down and then amended, "I mean, *fatter* girl group."

Valerie mumbled an insult through a mouthful of chocolate icing and cream filling.

"I did *not* have liposuction!" Alexandra exclaimed indignantly.

"Alexandra!" Alexander snapped impatiently. "Go wait in the car!"

"Make me, nose job."

"Implants."

"Penile—ow!"

Alexander had stomped on her foot to shut her up. The Cabot siblings had been raised to play rough.

Alexander smiled at the Pussycats. "So, ladies. How'd our set go?"

Josie glared at their so-called manager. "You'd know if you'd been there."

"Josie toes," Alexander said as if talking to a

child, "I'm running a management company here. I can't be everywhere at once."

"Ooh, wouldn't it be cool if you could, though?" Melody said. "I could be here . . . and in the living room. And in Japan! Eating ramen noodles!" Melody went to the doorway and began stepping in and out of the kitchen, testing her theory.

"Alexander, you have no other clients," Valerie pointed out. "Where else do you need to be?"

Alexander put his hands on his hips, exasperated. "On the street, spreading the Gospel of the Pussycats. Handing out flyers, working the masses, building a ground-swell . . ."

"Waiting in line for Du Jour tickets," Alexandra tattled.

The Pussycats looked at Alexander in disbelief.

"It's for business!" he said defensively. "I've got to check out the competition. . . . I mean, I don't even like Du Jour!"

Now the girls glowered at him.

Alexander gulped as he fumbled in his pocket for his cell phone and flipped it open. "Hello? Oh, hey . . . uh . . . man," he said a little too loudly. "You want a demo tape of The Pussycats? Sure, I'll hook you up, brother." He covered the phone with his hand and winked at the girls. "Guy who books all the big clubs. Wants to hear your tape."

"The phone didn't even ring," Josie pointed out.

"Uh—it's on vibrate," he said quickly. Then spoke into the phone. "Really? I should come over now? No problem. I'll be right there."

He blew the girls a kiss, then dashed out of the house.

Alexandra folded her arms and smiled at the girls. "You know he's lying."

"You know your fly's open," Josie said.

Alexandra glanced down. Blushing furiously, she quickly zipped up the expensive jeans. "You guys suck!" was the only thing she could think to say, and flounced out after her brother.

"Well, that's perfect," Valerie said morosely. "Even our manager would rather hear another band."

Suddenly Melody shouted at them from the living room. "You guys! Come here!"

Melody sounded terrified! Josie and Valerie dashed into the living room to see what was wrong. Melody stood transfixed in front of the TV. She was watching MTV—but she wasn't aghast at an offensive video. She was listening to MTV reporter Serena Altschul recount the details of a late-breaking news bulletin: ". . . We

37

have just received a confirmed report that the members of the pop group sensation Du Jour disappeared in their private jet today, vanishing from the radar forty miles east of the town of Riverdale."

The girls gasped as an image of Du Jour filled the screen.

"Authorities are still trying to determine the whereabouts of the plane," Serena continued, "and if there are indeed any survivors. Du Jour's label, MegaRecords, has yet to release a statement. But they *have* released a limited-edition commemorative boxed set—complete with a CD-ROM *History of Du Jour*—in stores tomorrow. We will keep you posted as to any further development in what seems to be yet another rock and roll tragedy."

Melody sank into a chair, her eyes brimming with tears. "Those poor, poor boys." But then brightened up. "But they didn't say they were dead!" She turned to her friends, her eyes full of hope. "Remember the time you guys thought *I* was missing, but I really just fell asleep in my closet?"

But Josie had a feeling these guys weren't asleep in anybody's closet. She stared at their faces in the photo. They were so young—smiling, posing, horsing around, on top of the world—totally oblivious to what awaited them in the near future.

*What a total, total bummer.* "Man, that is so sad," Josie murmured, shaking her head. "It makes you realize—it can all be over in a flash."

"I know." Valerie sighed. "At least they had a record deal."

"Val!"

Valerie shrugged.

Josie started to pace the threadbare carpet. Du Jour's plane going down was a total tragedy—even if she wasn't too crazy about their music. Sadly, there was nothing she or anybody else could do about it besides mourn their passing.

But wait—maybe there *was* something they could do. And maybe it was the only thing anyone could do when they looked into the eyes of death and thanked the heavens it wasn't their turn yet.

*We can live!*

But not just live the way most people did it— sleepwalking through life, dreaming of all the wonderful things they wanted to be or do, complaining about their crummy life . . . but never getting up off the couch long enough to change the channel.

Just when Josie's maniacal pacing began to get worrisome, she whirled around and faced her friends. "We *can* have a record deal. But we can't just sit here waiting for it to happen. Life's too short. We're musicians. We should be playing mūsic!"

"We *do* play," Valerie argued, slumping down on the couch. "Nobody cares."

Josie's eyes flashed. "*I* care."

Valerie and Melody sat up and exchanged a look of surprise. Josie was rockin'!

Josie paced in front of them like one of those guys selling "How to Be A Success" tapes on late-night infomercials. "If life gives you lemons, you make lemonade. When the going gets tough . . ."

"The tough make lemonade?" Melody suggested.

"What?" asked Valerie.

"Never mind!" Josie told her. "Come on— pack up your bass!" Full of new hope and inspiration, Josie grabbed her guitar case and headed for the front door.

*We don't have time to grovel in bowling alleys anymore, she thought. We're going to hit the streets, kick some butt—and make our dreams come true!*

# 4

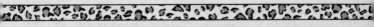

Once upon a time downtown Riverdale consisted of a single, quiet tree-lined street dotted with friendly Mom-and-Pop shops and markets, and even a hardware store that had been in the same family for four generations. Main Street was a place where a handshake was as good as a promise, and merchants knew their customers and all their children by their first names.

But Mom and Pop had long since moved to a retirement home, and Main Street Riverdale had been invaded by all of the trendiest chain-store shops a teenager could desire— Starbucks and Blockbuster, Abercrombie and Gap. Station wagons and jalopies had been replaced by SUVs, old-timers heading to the barbershop were now outnumbered by legions of shop-till-they-dropped teenagers buying all

JOSIE AND THE PUSSYCATS

the latest name-brand products their credit cards could handle.

One of the most impressive stores on the new strip was the multilevel MegaRecords Megastore, where kids could buy the most coveted thing of all: coolness.

Three girls bustled out of the store, their arms full of shopping bags, wearing identical pairs of brand-new pink shoes. One girl wore a Mylar balloon with the brand name tied to her wrist.

"I *live* for these pink shoes!" one of them squealed, holding out a foot to admire the new shoe in the sunlight.

"They're *so* much cooler than our *red* shoes!" her friend agreed.

The girl with the Mylar balloon froze in the middle of the sidewalk as a major new insight rocked her brain. "You guys!" she gasped. "*Pink* is the new *red*!"

Wyatt Frame, making his first trip down Main Street, stopped the girl with the Mylar balloon, and checked his hair in the refection of its silvery surface. *A well-dressed, well-groomed man is a confident man*, Wyatt thought, then let her go. Totally oblivious, the girls bustled on, completely absorbed by their purchases.

Wyatt walked into the MegaRecords Megastore and looked around. A DJ in headphones ruled from a small music center in the middle of the store, playing requests . . . which mostly meant any CDs the management wanted him to push.

Wyatt strode up to him and flashed his business card. "Wyatt Frame. MegaRecords. I'm scouting the area for local talent, and I was wondering if there's anyone worth hearing."

The DJ pulled up one side of headphones. "Saw the card, missed everything else. Start over while I change songs."

Wyatt laid a commanding hand on the DJ's arm. "Oh, no, wait—play this." He pulled a CD from his coat pocket and handed it to the man. "It's the new single from Du Jour. Recorded just a few days ago, right before . . ." Wyatt paused, to appear appropriately upset. "Before the . . . disappearance." He smiled at the DJ and shrugged. "I'd like to . . . test the reaction."

"Right on!" The DJ eagerly took the CD and loaded it into the player—hanging out in Riverdale, he'd never been the first to play anything. He leaned down to the mike and made the announcement: "Check it out, y'all! I've got the world premiere of the last single ever from the late Du Jour. Just for all you right here in the store!"

An excited murmur rippled through the store. Everyone—even the little old lady in the tiny country and western section—stopped to listen.

Seconds later, through the miracle of modern recording, the well-known voices of Du Jour sang out through the store's speakers, as if singing from beyond the grave:

> *"Du Jour 'round the world.*
> *Now and forever!*
> *Flyin' so high*
> *In all kinds of weather . . ."*

At first many of the kids seemed sad—a few cheerleaders even held each other and cried. But as the song played on, the teenagers all seemed to magically . . . perk up.

"I love this song!" one girl said.

"It's their best ever!" another cried.

Another girl gasped and her hand flew to her mouth. "If I don't buy it, everyone will absolutely *hate* me!"

Everyone in the store totally agreed.

Except for one girl. A rather unstylish girl, Wyatt noted, eyeing her outfit in disgust.

"That's just because they're mindless drones who will gobble up anything you tell them is cool," the girl said to Wyatt. She was browsing through a miniscule section of old school punk rock CDs.

Wyatt turned to her, and appeared captivated by her remarks. "I see. . . . Wow, you're *really* a free thinker, aren't you?"

The girl seemed surprised to get this reaction from anyone shopping in a MegaRecords Megastore. She'd expected him to ignore her and slowly move away. She smiled crookedly and nodded, sure of her superior music knowledge.

"Well, if you don't mind, I'd love to talk to you some more." Wyatt showed her his MegaRecords business card, and her eyes widened in feigned interest. "People in the recording industry always want to get the opinion of individuals like yourself," he explained. "You know, find out what you think we're doing wrong."

The girl laughed. "Yeah, right. How much time do you have?"

"As much as you want." He smiled like a crocodile.

Now the girl really was surprised. She usually shopped in alternative used vinyl stores, but maybe MegaRecords wasn't so bad after all. Not if they were willing to listen to what a real lover of music had to say. She followed him as he led her upstairs, toward his "office," . . . in the back of the store, through a door into the storage room . . . past large boxes of CDs.

As she trailed behind him, she was too busy thinking of all the great underappreciated bands she wanted to tell him about to notice that he was whispering into his shirt cuff, like some kind of secret agent.

"This must be my lucky day," Wyatt said, smiling, as he led her to the very back of the large storeroom and slid open a very large door. "A real nonconformist. I'm *sooo* interested to hear what else you have to say."

With visions of rockabilly dancing in her head the girl walked blindly through the open doorway into the back alley.

Out of nowhere a white unmarked van gunned down the alley and screeched to a halt right in front of her. Before she could even open her mouth, two men in black suits and shades jumped out, pulled her into the van, and then it sped away.

"Really?" Wyatt said as the van sped away. "Is that so?" Then he laughed. Well, getting rid of that loose cannon was easy enough.

Just then his cell phone rang. Still chuckling, he answered. "Cheerio!"

"I'm waiting. . . ."

The tone in the woman's voice wiped every

trace of a smile from Wyatt's face. He could hear her tapping her manicured nails on the polished desktop in her office, could clearly imagine the ferocious look on her beautiful face. "I-I'm on it, Fiona, I am, it's just . . . you wouldn't *believe* this place. It's a cultural wasteland. I mean, they only have *four* Starbucks!"

"*Stop making excuses and get your butt back here—with a band!*" she screamed.

"Tomorrow," Wyatt insisted. "You'll have a band first thing in the morning. I *swear!*"

"Good. Then you'll still have a job. . . . Maybe."

Wyatt winced as she slammed down the phone. Trembling, he pulled out a fine linen handkerchief and dabbed at the sweat that had broken out on his brow. Usually when Fiona said "Jump," Wyatt said "How high?"

But honestly, did the woman expect him to perform miracles? It wasn't as if he'd been dropped out of the sky into New York or L.A., where every other barrista and checkout clerk was an aspiring Kurt Cobain. He was in bloody Riverdale, for godsake . . . He wasn't even sure what state he was in!

Wyatt hurried through the crowded storeroom, straightened his jacket, then stepped back out into the store. He glanced around. No one had noticed him.

He looked at his expensive gold watch. It was almost evening—time was running out. He had no idea where to go, what to do, but he knew one thing—he had to keep moving.

He shoved past a crowd of kids and dashed out onto the sidewalk. He searched up and down the street for some kind of sign. Which way? Which way? He didn't have a clue. So he flipped a coin. Heads he'd go left, tails he'd go right.

He watched the coin fly in the air, then tumble back down, but when he tried to catch it, it slipped through his fingers. *Just my luck*, he sighed.

The coin rolled around and around on the sidewalk till Wyatt stomped it with his Italian loafer. Then he dropped to his knees and looked.

*Heads—left.*

Wyatt shrugged. *Left is good.*

He scooped up the quarter, got to his feet, then strode off down Main Street.

*Gotta find a new band—any band—now!*

Josie pulled her van up to the curb in the middle of Riverdale's Main Street and cut the motor. She'd dragged the band downtown to play their music—but not in any club, or even a bowling alley this time.

They were going to play right out here on the street. Raw and unplugged.

It was dark now, and the streetlamps and store lights flickered on, lending an air of fantasy to the night. Did the stars always twinkle so brightly, or was it the passion in Josie's heart that spangled the night sky? Josie had no idea what might happen, but she was ready to wail at the moon until the sun came up to summon the music gods' attention.

The Pussycats set up quickly in front of a popular store. Josie and Val were going acoustic and Melody had only brought her snare drum and hi-hat cymbal. Josie preferred the volume electricity provided, but tonight she felt as if she could make good music on a souvenir ukulele if she had to.

As Josie tuned her guitar, she glanced up across the street, where a couple of workmen were dismantling a huge billboard. A billboard that touted Du Jour as THE #1 BAND IN THE WORLD! The men had just torn down the words, leaving the illuminated larger-than-life faces of Du Jour smiling down from the heavens.

A lump formed in Josie's throat. So she thought their music sucked—so what? They had been fellow travelers in the Land of Music. "Hey, guys," she whispered, "wherever you are . . . this one's for you."

Then she shook off the sadness and turned to her two best friends. She was pumped. She was psyched! "Pussycats unplugged!" she cried. *"Here we go!"*

Valerie shook out her long dark hair, ready to rock. Melody beamed as she pounded out the opening beat: "One! Two! Three!"

Then Josie sang her heart out.

Only . . . three lines into the song the owner of the store came racing out to the sidewalk. "What do you think you're doing?" he shouted, waving his hands.

The Pussycats' music ground to a halt.

" 'Scuse me?" Josie asked politely.

"You can't play here!" he yelled. "I have things to sell! They're new! And orange!"

Josie frowned. "So?"

"So?" he sputtered. The man looked as if he was about to blow a gasket. "Look at you! You're . . ." He gave them the once-over, and his eyes were not kind. "Who's gonna come into my store with *you* outside!?"

"Last I checked it was a free country," Val argued.

"Yeah?" the man shouted. "Well, last I checked I was calling the cops!" With that he threw up his hands and stormed back into his shop.

The girls looked at one another, looked back at the shop, then scoffed.

"No way he's calling the cops," Josie said confidently.

The girls took up their instruments again. Melody raised her sticks to start the song over—

When the wail of a siren split the night.

Josie glanced down the street and spotted flashing red and blue lights. They must be chasing a speeder, or a drunk driver . . . They couldn't be coming this way. Surely . . .

The lights were headed the Pussycats' way.

There was no time to pack up their gear. No time to jump in the van and pray it started.

So Josie did the only thing she could do. She slung her acoustic guitar over her shoulder and used her vocal cords to the max to holler, "Run!"

Wyatt grumbled as he drove aimlessly through the streets of Riverdale. " 'Find a band, Wyatt'. . . ." he said, mocking Fiona's voice. " 'Find a band—now!' "

He'd given up walking and switched to his rented Jeep Navigator. He'd tuned in the nearest NPR station for some calming music— hanging out with Du Jour had made him a devoted classical music fan.

But this was all bloody ridiculous. How could you find something if it wasn't there?

"This is impossible!" he bellowed as he relentlessly drove on through the night. "Where the hell am I supposed to find a—"

He turned the corner.

Some people darted into the street.

Wyatt slammed on his brakes and screeched to a stop, expecting to hear the sound of bodies thudding against the massive hood of his car.

But miraculously . . . it appeared he hadn't hit anybody.

Wyatt gasped for breath and stared out his windshield at the idiots he'd almost killed.

Three girls stood frozen in the glare of the headlights like terrified deer. Three very hot girls, actually . . . Carrying instruments?

Wyatt cocked his head and studied them. As he did another car passed by, illuminating the girls in perfect spotlights. A bus backfired, sending a plume of smoke wafting across the scene.

To top it off, some workmen crossed the street carrying a piece of the dismantled Du Jour billboard, the piece that read: THE #1 BAND IN THE WORLD!

Mesmerized, his brain working overtime, Wyatt grabbed a clear empty CD case from the seat beside him. With trembling hands, he held it up to frame the image of the foxy girls standing amid the light and smoke in the middle of the night streets.

*Spectacular!*

The sound of a choir singing Beethoven's *Ode to Joy* rang through his mind.

Acting quickly, Wyatt turned off the Beethoven blaring from the radio, pushed the automatic window button to OPEN, then leaned out the window, offering his lovely prey his most charming smile—and one of his business cards. "Hello, ladies. Wyatt Frame, MegaRecords."

Would they run away screaming, frightened to be approached on the street at night? Would they tell him where to go and flip him the finger?

No, the redhead looked at her two friends, then cautiously reached for his card.

Wyatt held his breath. The girls were knockouts, all three of them. And he didn't give a bloody whit if they sounded like Miss Piggy in triplicate when they sang. The music they could always manipulate.

But he had to start with a look, an image, at least a tiny scrap of raw material out of which he could create a viable product.

Something in his gut—or perhaps other parts of his anatomy—told him these girls had what it took.

*I think I've found my band*, he thought with a delicious smile.

Just wait until he called Fiona.

A few minutes later Josie, Valerie, and Melody sat down in a Starbucks with Wyatt Frame. They weren't sure what to make of the slick guy yet, but he was treating them to any coffee they wanted and the baked good of their choice, so they decided to at least hear him out.

After all, if nothing else, he'd rescued them from a nasty encounter with the Riverdale police.

"Well," Wyatt said, beaming at them as they sipped their café au laits and lattes. "I can't tell you how pleased I am to be at a table with the Pussyhats."

Josie choked on her foam. "Uh, that's Pussy*cats*."

Wyatt stopped, confused, then nodded. "Of course. Of course. That explains why you're not wearing any."

Now the girls looked confused.

"Hats," he explained. "Anyway," he continued, leaning across the table, "the point is, I speak for everyone at the label when I say we'd *love* to have you sign with MegaRecords."

"Wait! Don't sign anything!"

Josie turned in her chair. Why wasn't she

surprised to see Alexander Cabot and his sister Alexandra bursting through the door? It was like their manager had radar for anything that even remotely had anything to do with signing them for a paying job.

Wyatt frowned condescendingly. "Who are you?"

"Alexander Cabot. I'm the Pussycats' manager."

"Well, then," Wyatt remarked, "I guess you're entitled to fifteen percent of whatever they make."

Alexander gasped like a landed trout for a moment, then grabbed Josie by the shoulders. "Sign everything!"

Taking a deep breath, Alexander dragged a chair over to the tiny table and squeezed in next to Wyatt Frame—his new best friend.

Alexandra—*Like does she always go wherever her brother goes?* Josie wondered—managed to snuggle up to Wyatt on his other side. "I'm his sister, Alexandra," she said, actually batting her eyes flirtatiously at the man. "*Love* the accent," she added, then attempted to adopt an English accent herself. "I used to summer on the Continent. Fancy a snog?"

Josie's mind was trying to keep up with all this, but the Cabots were distracting her from what she thought she'd heard Wyatt say. "Wait, hold up!" she ordered everyone. She looked at Wyatt suspiciously. "You want to sign us?"

Wyatt nodded, pleased with himself.

Josie couldn't believe what she was hearing. "But you've never even heard us play."

"Oh. I'm sorry," Wyatt said sarcastically, and pretended to be confused. "I thought you were in a rock band that *wanted* to sign with a major record label." He clucked his tongue and shoved back his chair. "I guess I was wrong. . . ." He started to stand up.

"No!" all five Riverdale kids cried out.

Wyatt cocked his head and considered them, then sat back down with a smirk on his face.

"I just didn't know it could happen this fast!" Josie explained.

"Well, that's the music biz for you," Wyatt said philosophically. "If you wait for it to slow down, it just might pass you by. Look what happened to the Beastie Boys."

"But they're huge stars," Valerie said.

Wyatt smiled smugly. "I know."

Josie found that answer even more perplexing, but she let it go. She pushed her chair back and tried to catch Valerie's eye.

" 'Scuse me, I gotta . . . you know, ladies' room."

She gave Val a little nudge. "Oh! Yeah. Me, too."

They both stood and looked at Melody.

Melody smiled sweetly. "I went before we left." She turned to Wyatt. "You know, before you leave the house, you should always try. Even if you don't have to—"

Valerie grabbed Melody by the arm and dragged her away from the table.

Wyatt sat back in his chair and watched them, wary.

Josie waited until they had all squeezed into the rest room. It was the tiniest Josie had ever been in. You'd think in a place that pumped this much liquid, they'd have a larger facility. The girls huddled up against the sink for a quick Pussycats meeting.

"Okay, this is crazy—" Josie began.

Just then the door swung open, and Alexandra Cabot elbowed her way toward the mirror. "Gotta gloss!"

Then the door opened again, and Alexander squeezed in. Now it was totally claustrophobic.

"Alexander!" Josie exclaimed.

"Are you having a band meeting?" he asked. "If it's a band meeting, I should be here!"

"It's the ladies' room!" Josie complained.

"Nothing I haven't seen before," he replied, stubbornly folding his arms and planting himself next to the paper towel dispenser.

Valerie dug around in her shoulder bag. "Anyone have change for a tampon?"

Alexander blanched. "I'll be outside."

But no matter what they said or did, Alexandra stood her ground, pretending to look busy trying out "famous" faces in the mirror.

Josie looked at her buddies. They couldn't stay in here all night—Wyatt Frame would get suspicious. He might even leave! At last the girls gave up and did their best to ignore Miss Britney Wannabe.

"How cool is this?" Valerie said, barely able to contain her excitement. "MegaRecords!"

But Josie shook her head. "And you don't think any of this is just the tiniest bit strange?"

"Like what?" Melody says.

"Well, like that Wyatt guy out there, for one."

"Oh, yeah," Melody said, nodding her head in understanding. "Like how he ordered a triple cappuccino but scooped off all the foam? Why not just get espresso? Plus, how he keeps folding his napkin like he's afraid he doesn't have any real friends, just people who want to use him because he's some big music guy?"

The girls all stopped and thought about that for a moment.

"Yeah," Josie said, "but I was talking more about the whole record contract thing. It's super sudden—"

"But you said it, Josie!" Val insisted. "You said we had to get out of the house and make things happen for ourselves. Well—we did!"

"I know, I know!" Josie agreed. She was worried, and tried to pace, but couldn't because there wasn't any room. "I just think we should think about it for a second . . ."

Valerie and Melody nodded. They all stood silent for a second, thinking.

Then their eyes met . . .

And all three began to scream and hug and jump up and down. When they managed to settle down, they did their pussycat handshake.

Alexandra looked over her shoulder at them in the mirror, her face filled with envy. Then she blotted her lips and did what any well-bred upper-class young lady would do: offer a fake congrats. "Gee, how exciting for you, Josie. You'll get to go away and make a record." She smiled and smoothed her clothes down over her curves for effect. "And poor Alan M. will have to stay behind in Riverdale. All alone . . . with me."

Josie glared at her. Out of all the people in Riverdale, why did Alexandra have to be the one to figure out she had a secret crush on Alan M.? And Josie didn't doubt for a minute that the girl would follow up on her threat to go after him while she was gone.

But what could Josie do? How could she choose between the two loves of her life?

# 5

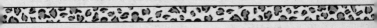

"I can't believe they let you fly me to the city with you. . . ." Alan M. said the next morning as he sat next to Josie in MegaRecords' private jet. Wyatt was flying Josie and the other Pussycats—plus Alexander and Alexandra—to sign their recording contract.

Alan M. gazed out the window and shook his head, totally impressed. "You know what this means, don't you, Josie? It means they think you're gonna be huge!"

"Shhh!" Josie said. "I had to tell them you're my guitar tech." She glanced toward the back of the plane at Alexandra, who sat there steaming. Beside her, Alexander was reading *The Operator: David Geffen Builds, Buys, and Sells the New Hollywood.* "I still don't see why *you* had to come along," he taunted his sister.

Alexandra stared wistfully at Alan M. "I'm here because I was in the comic book."

"What?"

"Nothing."

Meanwhile, Valerie and Melody were lounging on two very plush reclining seats. Josie got up to join them and plopped down on Val's lap.

"Ooof! What's up, fatty?"

Josie pinched her. "Shut up!" she said, laughing.

Melody sighed in delight. "You know how people always say, 'This is the life'?"

Her friends nodded.

"Well, I think this is when they say it!"

The Pussycats laughed.

"Private plane," Valerie said.

"Record deal," Josie added.

Melody played with the nozzle on the ceiling over their heads. "Air!"

"Loads of cash . . ." Val pulled her wallet from her purse and opened it to show that it was empty. "Oops. Scratch that. Still poor." But then she pulled out a small plastic rectangle. "But at least I won't need this anymore."

It was her Riverdale Muni bus pass. She studied the picture and cracked up. "God, this picture!"

Josie pulled out her own bus pass and held it up. "I love this picture!"

"Yeah," said Valerie. "'Cause you look good in it. I look like a broccoli. Or the Keebler Tree. L'il elves makin' cookies in my hair . . ."

Melody studied her own bus pass. "You look great. You know, this is the only bus pass in Muni history with three people in the picture."

"It's not my fault," Josie said. "You both jumped in mine."

"Oh, yeah, right," Valerie replied, laughing. "*You* both jumped in *mine!*"

"You know what?" Josie said softly, holding up her bus pass. "We should keep these. Remind us where we came from."

"My parents already told me I came from the stork," Melody said. "But then I found this book under their bed . . . Well, let's just say it's a whole different story." She nodded knowingly.

Josie grinned and shook her head. There was nobody else in the world like Melody, that was for sure. Or Valerie. *And I'm one lucky girl to have them for friends*, she realized. And there was no one she'd rather have by her side as she headed off on this wild adventure. Who knew where they'd be a week, a month, a year from now? She was sure glad she wasn't going alone.

"Let's promise something. Right here," she told her two best friends. "That no matter what happens, if we become huge stars, or if we wind up on one of those VH-1 Specials where we're walking on the beach all bald and sad music is playing but we lie and say we're much happier *not* being huge stars?"

Val and Melody nodded. They knew exactly what she meant.

"Let's promise that we'll always be friends," Josie declared. "Friends first, and a band second."

"Friends first," said Valerie.

"Friends first," Melody agreed.

"Swear on your bus pass," Josie insisted.

They dropped their bus passes on a snack table and solemnly piled up their hands, one on top of the other. "I swear on my bus pass," they all chanted at once.

They all laughed and stuffed their civilian keepsakes back into their bags.

Then Josie, who'd never been on an airplane before, leaned in and whispered, "Okay, real stuff? Anyone like, majorly disappointed here? I mean, I always heard if you went on an airplane they gave a little bag of free peanuts."

Melody nodded.

"Yeah, it sucks, man," Valerie complained.

Just then a private flight attendant walked by.

The girls looked up hopefully.

But the woman only held up a towel and a

bottle of scented body oil. "Can I offer any of you a full body massage?" she asked.

Disappointed, the girls sank back in their seat. "Nah."

Meanwhile, Wyatt Frame had been standing in front of a large mirror, a mirror exactly like the one that the members of Du Jour had used just the day before to admire their own Pure Platinum tips and sexy sneers. But Wyatt's conscience, if it even existed anymore, had a very high threshold and he felt absolutely no remorse. In fact, the only thing worrying him right now was which tie to wear with today's outfit. He wanted to look smashing when he arrived in Fiona's office to accept her praise for his miraculous discovery. He held up one tie after the other, but he just couldn't decide. He decided to take a break and check on the pilot and find out the ETA.

First he glanced at the Riverdale kids to make sure there were no little fires to put out. Everyone looked relatively happy, except for that Alexandra broad. She looked like trouble. But for the rest of them—they were remarkably polite and undemanding for kids who were headed for unbelievable fame and fortune.

*Just wait*, he thought. Then he quickly

slipped into the cockpit and shut the door behind him.

The pilot took one look at him, sighed, and
stood up to begin strapping on his parachute.

"No, no, it's all right, Lex," Wyatt said, waving him back into his seat. "We're not going to
have any problems with these girls."

The pilot relaxed and took over the controls
again. "Enjoy your flight, sir," he said.

Wyatt laughed like a *Scooby Doo* villain. "Oh,
I will, Lex. Believe me, this time I will."

# 6

Josie blinked—and her life was transformed.

As soon as they got to the city, Wyatt rushed them off to a hundred appointments.

They had their hair cut, highlighted, and styled by hairdressers it took months to get an appointment with.

They had their makeup done by the top artists in the city—high-priced experts who only had time for faces destined for the cover of *People* magazine.

They had their own clothing stylists ready to help them find the perfect look. They had racks and racks of designer duds, clothes that the Pussycats quickly personalized by attacking them with scissors and pins.

The stylists were horrified—at first. Until they saw how hot the girls looked in their one-of-a-kind outfits. The stylists scribbled notes and took pictures—kids would be buying these new styles off the racks within weeks.

Out on the street, the girls could hardly believe how fabulous they looked.

"Pinch me," Josie told Valerie.

"What?"

"Pinch me! I need to know if this is all real!"

Val and Mel pinched her—hard.

"Ow!" she squealed. Then she grinned at her friends. "It's real!"

Then they all squealed.

"Ready, glamour girls?"

Wyatt appeared like magic to whisk them away in a sleek black limo stocked with their favorite snacks and sodas . . . and those little bags of peanuts they didn't get on the plane.

But as Josie started to get in, she had the strangest feeling, like somebody was staring at her. She glanced up at a towering sky-scraper and froze. "Whoa . . ." she whispered.

Her face—a huge Josie face—smiled down from a new billboard that was just being painted on the side of the building. And the headline read:

TOMMY HILFIGER INTRODUCES MEGARECORDS'
JOSIE AND THE PUSSYCATS!

"Jeez," Josie said. "That's so . . . huge."

Wyatt smiled and laid a hand on her shoulder. "This is just the beginning," he cooed in her ear.

Josie knew she ought to feel wonderful. She ought to be shouting her heart out. But instead she just felt . . . creepy. Like she'd won something by cheating. "But are you sure you should be putting that up already?" she asked Wyatt. "I mean, we haven't even recorded anything yet. What if you don't like it?" Her hands flew to her face as an even more horrifying thought crossed her mind. "What if *nobody* likes it?"

"Oh, I wouldn't worry about that," Wyatt reassured her. "Besides, if you screw up, we'll just put somebody else up there!" He laughed uproariously as he gave her a gentle push into the limo.

Josie gulped as she slid into her seat. Did every rising star feel like this—like a fake just waiting to be unmasked? She scooted over to the window and tried to peer up for another look. *Oh, man.* . . . She never felt sure of her looks, hated to look at pictures of herself, and here they'd gone and plastered a whole building with her giant grinning face. *At least they airbrushed all the zits*, she thought miserably. She sneaked another look. *And my teeth look really white.* . . .

Josie was so busy studying her picture she didn't realize Valerie and Melody were still standing outside on the street, staring at the billboard with a different point of view.

"They got our name wrong," Val said.

Wyatt frowned at her. "Hmm?"

Valerie shook her head. "Our name," she repeated, pointing at the sign. "We're not 'Josie and the Pussycats.' We're just 'The Pussycats.'"

Wyatt sighed as if dealing with an unruly child. "Josie's the singer," he explained patiently. "The public needs someone out front to identify with."

"Hmph!" Valerie didn't buy it.

"Trust me," Wyatt insisted. "Our studies show that bands with the word *and* in their name sell twice as many records as those that don't."

Valerie jammed her fists on her hips. "Since when? What about the Beatles? Or the Rolling Stones? Or the Backstreet Boys?"

"Well! If you want to split hairs . . ." Wyatt shrugged. "But think about it, Valerie. Are you more interested in a band called simply 'The Pussycats'? Or . . . are you more likely to buy a CD, read a comic, watch a cartoon, go see a movie about a trio of luscious ladies called 'Josie and the Pussycats'?"

Melody cocked her head thoughtfully. "It does have a ring to it," she admitted.

Wyatt shot Valerie a look that said *So there* as he helped Melody into the limo.

But Val still stood there, staring up at the outlandish billboard—specifically at the two tiny silhouettes of girls in ears and tails playing bass and drums way in the background. "So, are the little ones supposed to be Mel and me?" she complained. " 'Cause I don't even have a face!"

She turned to Wyatt.

But Wyatt was gone. He was in the limo with the other girls . . .

The limo that was pulling away from the curb without her!

"Hey!" Val ran after it, shouting and waving her arms.

At last it jerked to a halt. The window rolled down, and Wyatt popped his head out. "Oh! Sorry, Val. We had no idea you weren't in here."

Valerie scowled and hurried to catch up, re-peating a line from her anger management book as she ran: "My fists are not my friends. . . ." As soon as she slipped into the backseat, the driver hit the gas.

* * *

Across the street a dark figure hiding in the shadows watched the girls get into their chariot and drive off. And it was not until the car had completely vanished into the noisy night traffic that the figure slowly limped away.

# 7

"What did I tell you, Fiona? They're perfect."
Wyatt was in the gym the next morning doing
crunches on a gravity bar as he talked to his
boss on his cell phone headset.

Actually Wyatt wasn't really doing the
crunches. Two muscular trainers he'd paid
were pushing him up and down on the bar.

"Only girls show up for the boy bands," Wyatt told Fiona. "But this way guys will come
out to see the hot chicks in tight leopard outfits,
and girls will still show up because they'll idol-
ize these babes.

"Imagine Christina Aguilera times three. Except one of them is really tan." He stopped and
thought a minute. "Or TLC with two white
chicks . . . Oh, or Hole, without the skinny
blond guy, and Courtney Love's got red hair
instead of—"

"Wyatt!" Over at MegaRecords headquarters, Fiona was getting impatient. "I get it without the stupid analogies."

Just then a conservative-looking man in a gray suit poked his head in Fiona's doorway. He pointed emphatically at his watch.

Still listening on the phone, Fiona waved him into her office. "Put them in the studio tomorrow," she told Wyatt over the phone. "We'll talk later. The feds are here with some foreigners, and I've got to give them the tour."

"You won't be disappointed," Wyatt told her.

"I'd better not be," Fiona shot back. "We can't afford another Du Jour disaster."

As she hung up the phone, the man in the gray suit ushered in a group of very serious-looking men, representatives from many different nations in the world. Definitely not tourists.

Fiona swiveled in her chair to face them.

Some of the men gasped. Fiona, the head of MegaRecords, was one of the most beautiful women they had ever seen. And the look on her face was twice as deadly.

"Welcome, gentlemen," she said briskly. "Up until now our mutual friend from the State Department has shown you our 'legitimate' operations. And I'm sure you're wondering why

Agent Kelly and the United States government would be paying so much money to what appears to be a record company."

There was a murmur of agreement among the visitors.

"Well," Fiona announced, "I'm about to show you why." She reached for a shiny music award on her desk. But instead of showing it off to her guests, she flipped open the top, revealing a large red button. When she pressed the button, the whole room jolted, startling the visitors, who reached for each other.

Fiona just laughed as the room began to move, slowly at first, then descending like a giant elevator. The view of the city through the wraparound windows disappeared as the room sank deeper and deeper into a warehouse-sized room. When her office hit bottom, she stood up and opened a door.

The delegates peered over her shoulder in amazement, totally intrigued by this secret James Bond-like room.

"This is what our operation *really* does," Fiona informed them. "From this command center we control the most influential demographic of the population. . . ."

She led the men out onto a catwalk, which gave them a marvelous view of the goings-on below. It was like a government War Room, only here instead of maps and satellite images, they could see huge screens showing music videos, fashion shows, and clips of famous celebrities. Dozens of work teams scurried from one work station to the next, sharing information and delivering results of tests.

"We decide everything," Fiona explained without the slightest trace of guilt. "From what clothes are in style, to what slang is en vogue."

Below them a team wearing FBI-style windbreakers with the word FASHION emblazoned across the back gathered around a mannequin showcasing a new outfit. "I'm thinking yellow Mylar jumpsuits with exposed midriffs. Kind of 'Pokemon' meets Jennifer Aniston."

"Mylar is the new leather!" one of the crew exclaimed.

The entire Fashion Team applauded.

Over in another area, the Slang Team was trying to coin a new term. "The new word for cool will be jerkin'," the team leader announced.

"Can you use that in a sentence, sir?" a team member asked.

"Certainly. Jerkin'—as in 'Those new Hilfiger jeans are totally jerkin'!"

"I like it," another slang-maker said. "It sounds dirty. Let's have Will Smith start saying it in public."

They all scribbled notes on their clipboards.

Smiling, Fiona led the group down a spiral staircase to the floor. "From what TV shows are popular . . ." She paused to hear that team's conversation.

"Can we squeeze another year out of *Friends*?"

"We'll have to kill David Schwimmer's movie career."

"Done and done."

". . . to which obviously straight celebrities are rumored to be gay . . ."

"Keanu Reeves!"

"Justin Timberlake!"

"Bryant Gumble!"

The whole rumor mill stopped and stared at him.

Another guy shrugged. "I'd buy that."

The team went back to shouting out other possibilities.

Fiona led her visitors to a huge video wall. "But how, you may ask, can our operation be so effective? Sure, these kids have brains like Play-Doh, just waiting to be molded into shape, but still, something else has to be going on, right?" She smiled at one of the delegates.

The delegate gave her a thumbs-up.

"To answer some of your questions," Fiona

continued, "we've produced a short educational film. *Lights!*"

Instantly the lights dimmed, and the delegates sat down in Imax-style seats that had been rolled in front of the video wall.

A film began to roll with a voiceover by the guy from Moviefone. The delegates sat lulled by his soothing and informative presentation.

"Rock and roll music," the voice said. "Now, it's as American as apple pie and color TV. But not so long ago, it was considered dangerous. A bad influence on the young people of this nation."

Now the monitors on the video wall around the main screen flicked on, showing a montage of rock and roll acts and screaming teens. Everything from the Beatles and Woodstock to the Sex Pistols and N'Sync . . .

"But eventually," the voice went on, "we realized that this rabid obsession with rock music could be used to our advantage. All the government has to do is plant subliminal messages inside the music to control the thought patterns of the youth of America."

Now the image on the screen showed a clean-cut girl and guy from the fifties, listening to music on a hi-fi. The animated words SUBLIMINAL MESSAGES floated out of the speakers, hitting the kids in waves. Their eyes

turned to swirling spirals. They smiled, hyp-
notized.

"Unlike the adult mind," the Moviefone guy
explained, "which is already loyal to certain
brands and styles, kids have an unlimited
amount of space to fill with new products and
fads, thus creating an entire demographic of eager consumers."

Two diagrams of the adult and teenage minds
flashed on the screen. "If we constantly change
fads and fashions, teens feel compelled to keep
up by buying new clothes and music and basically anything they think adults won't like. . . ."

Hundreds of brand names marched across
the screen.

"So all the while, they think they're being cool
and rebellious"—the voice laughed wickedly—
"but they're really keeping our entire economy
afloat!"

The screen filled with money raining down
on two very happy teens.

"So God bless the American teenager, and
rock music," movie man said. "And God bless
the United States of America, the most ass-
kickin' country in the world!"

As the lights came up again, MegaRecords' invited guests began to talk about what they'd
just heard.

"Where can we sign up?" the Japanese delegate asked eagerly.

"Right on the dotted line," Fiona replied.

An assistant handed out the contracts. Many of the delegates signed them immediately.

"But how can you control de rock bands?" the German delegate asked. "Vat if dey find out about ze hidden messages in der music?"

Fiona hit another button on her remote control. The video wall filled with images of rock stars—all of them dead or completely washed up: Elvis, Buddy Holly, Jimi Hendrix, Janis Joplin, Keith Moon, Hammer, Milli Vanilli, Leif Garrett, Tiffany, George Michael, Billy Ray Cyrus, Cat Stevens, the list went on and on.

"Ever wonder why so many rock stars die in plane crashes?" Fiona asked. "Overdose on drugs? We've been doing this a long time, gentlemen. If they start to get curious, our options are endless. Bankruptcies, shocking scandals, religious conversion. We've created a highly rated TV show just to explain what happens to these people." She clicked the remote again to an episode of VH-1's *Behind the Music*, the show that told the story of music industry has-beens.

The woman from Sri Lanka nodded her head. "I loved the one on Leif Garrett."

Satisfied, the German delegate joined the others in applause.

Fiona threw back her head and laughed, a deep, sexy, villainous laugh. *How wonderful to be adored.*

# 8

We're a long way from the old garage, Josie thought the next day as they arrived at the studio.

It was the day she'd always dreamed of—today she and her friends would record their very first CD.

"Wow," she said as they entered the studio and looked around at all the high-tech equipment. Josie didn't even know what most of it did. She hoped she wouldn't make a fool of herself during the recording session.

Melody was running around pushing on the foam soundproof walls. "The walls are mushy!" she squealed. She mashed herself up against the wall. "Oooh!"

"We brought some equipment in," Wyatt said as he came in behind them. "I assume it's all to your liking."

The girls rushed over to inspect their shiny instruments.

Josie lifted up a glossy white guitar. "Oh, my god—this is brand-new!"

"Can we play instruments that aren't used?" Val joked. "Think we'll know how?"

All the girls laughed.

Melody discovered a strange illuminated console. "I like this. It's got shiny knobs." She started to fiddle with them, but Wyatt suddenly rushed over and lifted her hands away.

"Oh, no, no, no. That we never touch," he told her firmly. "It's only the most expensive piece of equipment in the studio."

Josie and Valerie came over to look. Every wire in the studio seemed to run through this thing.

"It's the MegaSound 3000," Wyatt said. "Although the name sounds rather ominous, it's actually just a high-tech processor."

"How does it work?" Val asked.

"Why do you need to know that?" Wyatt replied, almost defensively.

Val chuckled "What, is it a big secret or something?"

The girls teased Wyatt good-naturedly, "Oooh. Wyatt's got a secret machine. He loves it . . . !"

Wyatt looked nervous at first, but then he

quickly recovered. "It's not a secret. I'll show you." He flipped some switches, and the machine hummed to life. "Girls, play a little something, will you?"

Josie and her friends picked up their instruments and began to play the first two lines of their new song "3 Small Words."

"It took six whole hours," Josie sang, "and five long days . . ."

Wyatt was stunned—the girls could actually sing! Their music sounded great, too—grungy and raw.

Wyatt motioned for them to stop. "Perfect. Now it'll just take a moment. . . ." He fiddled with the buttons on the MegaSound 3000 until a light hummed, then turned green.

"Now I'll play it back for you with the Mega-Sound." He hit another button, and the song played again.

The girls stopped what they were doing to stare, and listen.

The Pussycats sounded punched-up. Loud like a pop song, with thick production, special effects, and even a few backup vocals thrown in.

"Is that us?" Val asked.

Josie wasn't sure she liked the new sound. "It sounds so . . . so big. And . . . different."

"Of course it does," Wyatt said. "You've

never heard your music professionally produced before."

Seeing that the girls still looked confused, Wyatt explained. "It's kind of like when you hear your own voice on an answering machine. That sounds different, right?"

"I want a Big Mac," Melody suddenly blurted out.

Everyone stared at her.

"What? But, Mel," Valerie said, "you're a vegetarian."

"I know. But I suddenly want one. Maybe on the way back to the hotel?"

Val nodded. "Okay. As long as we can swing by a Foot Locker, too. I'm dying for a pair of old-school Tretorns."

"Jerkin'," Josie replied. "Tretorns are the new Adidas."

Josie's hand flew to her mouth. *What am I saying?* She looked at Val and Mel—they looked as puzzled by this conversation as she was. It was as if someone else were putting words in their mouths. But that was impossible.

"All this talk about food and shopping!" Wyatt snorted impatiently. "Should I drop you girls back at the Riverdale Mall or are you ready to make a record?"

"Hey, we're ready," Josie insisted. The girls quickly set up and tuned their instruments, and even put on their ears and tails. No one who listened to the record would know they were wearing them, but the Pussycats would.

Huddled over Melody's drum kit, the girls did a Pussycat handshake.

"This is it," Josie said. "Let's put it on wax."

All three smiled at each other. Their dreams were about to come true.

Melody counted off with her sticks. "ONE! TWO! THREE!"

And then the Pussycats ripped into the song.

From his spot in the booth, Wyatt actually looked impressed and began to bob his head in time with the music. Alexander had arrived and was dancing to the music like he was partying at Studio 54 in 1977. Alexandra rolled her eyes at the whole ridiculous scene . . . because she felt so left out.

But Josie didn't see any of them—she was too lost in the music, weaving a story with her two best friends in the world, and all the hopes and dreams they'd had since the first day they began this band seemed to resonate through every note. Josie and the Pussycats were having the time of their lives, and it showed in their music.

And as they sang, the machines—the technology—recorded it all . . . and turned it into something else entirely.

Over in the corner a tiny green light blinked on the Megasound 3000, indicating that the machine was silently and efficiently doing its job.

Standing in the sound booth, Wyatt Frame saw, and smiled.

The next couple of days were almost a blur. While the CDs were being pressed, Wyatt danced the girls through the hoops that came with being a rising star.

They had a photo shoot, with dozens of outrageously expensive outfits to try on. The girls giggled like little girls in a playhouse, and Josie thought it was just like playing dress-up, but she was blown away by the sophisticated images the photographer created from their amateurish poses.

They shot a video in one day—playing on the deck of a ship in outer space. By that evening it was wowing thousands of kids in MegaRecords stores around the country—introducing them to the sound of Josie and the Pussycats—and convincing them to buy the CD.

"This is the best CD ever!" one new Josie fan exclaimed after hearing only a few seconds of the music.

"Yeah," said another kid, "and I want some Gatorade."

"Gatorade is the new Snapple!" his buddy pointed out.

The buzz had started.

Out in the streets a fan actually stopped the Pussycats and asked for an autograph. The girls were thrilled! *Now we've really made it*, Josie thought.

Gap stores moved their racks of brand-new faux leopard-skin vests into the front windows.

All across America workers in stores were unpacking boxes loaded with Josie and the Pussycats candy, action figures, hair accessories, and even an all-access biography of the band.

All the while the band's single quietly climbed to #32 on the charts.

A young girl on the street recognized Melody. She pointed and screamed. Melody was so nervous, she wasn't sure what to do. So she pointed and screamed, too.

Within days Josie and the Pussycat merchandise began to sell out. Especially after the girls' *Rolling Stone* magazine cover hit the stands.

And then it happened—mere days, mere hours after recording the CD. Wyatt came to their hotel room with the latest copy of *Billboard* magazine. Josie, Val, and Melody huddled together to read the latest:

Their song "Pretend to Be Nice" had reached #1!

At first there was dead silence—as if all the air had been sucked out of the room. Then the Pussycats were screaming and hugging and leaping around.

"This must be a misprint," Alexandra said as she read it for herself.

Alexander, dressed in a white suit, platinum chains, and sunglasses, popped a bottle of champagne to congratulate himself on being the best band manager in the world.

Wyatt stood in the corner watching, amused. He kind of liked this stage of the game. It was sort of like being the fairy godmother at the moment when Cinderella, dressed in her sparkling new gown, realized she was actually going to the ball.

Finally Josie tried to calm down. "Okay. Okay. Okay, wait. Doesn't anybody else think it's kinda strange that this has all happened in a week?"

Wyatt's jaw dropped. He suddenly looked very nervous.

"No . . ." Val replied, still giddy.

But Josie continued. "And how all of a sudden we're on TV and in magazines, and we've never even played in front of an audience?"

Valerie stopped jumping and thought about it. "Yeah. That is strange."

Wyatt backed away, his hand reaching for the phone.

"Yeah," Melody agreed. "And you know what else is strange? Sometimes I look at my toes and I see a family of astronauts all lined up in a row."

Josie and Val stared at Mel for a beat. Then they all pulled off their shoes and stared at their toes.

Melody made the sound of a rocket and lifted her foot slowly up, up, up . . . as Josie and Val watched, nodding.

Wyatt picked up the phone. . . .

"Okay," Valerie said, getting back to Josie's original question. "But maybe this isn't strange at all. I mean, isn't this how it always happens? Some band you never heard of comes out of nowhere and suddenly gets huge for no apparent reason. Think about it. I mean, maybe it only seems strange because this time . . . the number-one band is *us*!"

The girls looked at each other and realized it was true. *They were* the number one band!

The screaming and hugging started all over again.

Wyatt let out a huge breath of air . . . and hung up the phone.

Just then there was a knock on the door. "Did

anybody order room service?" Josie asked as she went to the door.

"I hope somebody did!" Valerie said.

But when Josie opened the door, it wasn't any of the hotel staff. It was three highlighted girls dressed head to toe in pussycat. They pointed at Josie and jumped up and down, screaming.

"Who *are* you?" Josie asked.

When Melody got up and came over to the door, the girls in the hall started screaming, "Oh my god! It's Melody!"

Melody turned to Josie. "This keeps happening to me."

"Hey, we know them!" Valerie said.

Josie made a face. "Ew. We do?"

The girls squealed. Girl #1 managed to say, "We love you! We're your biggest fans!"

Now Josie remembered. They were the girls who had definitely not been their fans a few days ago. The ones who'd thrown a Diet Coke can at her van. "No, you hate us."

"Are you crazy?!" gasped Girl #2. "You're our new all-time favorite band of all time!"

"Josie and the Pussycats are the new Du Jour!" squealed Girl #3.

Girl #1 grinned: "Want us to prove it? Want to see our pussycat tattoos?!"

Giggling, all three girls turned around and started to drop their pants.

Freaked, Josie slammed the door. From out in the hall she heard: "We're sleeping out here!"

"Okay," Josie said to her friends. "That was way too weird."

Wyatt came over to join them. "Weird? Girls, what's the point of being famous if the people you hated in high school don't want to suck up to you? You're lucky. Most people have to wait until their ten-year high school reunion for revenge like that."

Wyatt stared out the window, suddenly bitter. The girls looked at him oddly. But then Wyatt made himself snap out of it. "Look," Wyatt said. "You're just going to have to get used to people throwing themselves at you. Speaking of throwing . . ."

He reached into his jacket. "Fiona, the head of MegaRecords, is throwing a huge party tonight in your honor—to celebrate all things Josie!"

Josie squirmed at the way he phrased that.

Smiling like Santa, Wyatt handed Josie and Mel one of the precious invitations.

"Uh . . . Wyatt?" Valerie said. "Where's mine?"

Puzzled, Wyatt searched his pockets, but then held out empty hands. Nothing. "That's odd," he said. "Well, why don't you come along, too? There's always room for one more."

Alexander and Alexandra stepped up.

"How about us?" Alexandra said.

"No," said Wyatt, and turned back to his megastars.

Josie looked at her invitation. It had a big picture of her face on the front. "A party," she said, trying to stay positive. "That's . . . kinda cool."

"Yes," Wyatt agreed. "But is it more cool than playing a stadium concert?" Then he gasped and covered his mouth. "Oops. I promised Fiona she could tell you."

"We're playing a stadium concert?" Josie asked.

Wyatt grinned now that the cat was out of the bag. "Next weekend."

Josie looked stunned. "Next weekend? . . . But shouldn't we play some small clubs first? Do some gigs in Europe? Build a following?"

"You *have* a following." Wyatt shook his head. "Honestly, J., I wouldn't send you out there if I didn't think you could deliver. It'd only make me look bad. I mean, this is the whole deal. Simultaneous pay-per-view Web cast, live streaming video. I'm sure your band-mates are très excited. Right, Melly Mel?"

"Our first concert ever!" she said. "Thanks, Wyatt!" She gave him a great big hug. Wyatt held on a little too long.

Still not letting go, Wyatt said, "Don't thank me, thank Fiona. It was all her idea. It's been part of her plan for you guys from the start. . . ."

# 9

"This is Operation Big Concert!" Fiona announced to a group of federal agents in the MegaRecords control room. "Where we finally take things to the next level! Isn't that right, Agent Kelly?"

Agent Kelly hesitated, unsure of what to say. Fiona glared.

"Uh, well, it sounds good, Fiona," Agent Kelly said diplomatically. "It's just . . . well, usually we use more *covert* code names. Maybe something like 'Operation Rolling Thunder' would be more appropriate."

Fiona made a face. "No. That's stupid!"

Kelly nodded and stepped back in line.

"When Josie and the Pussycats play their stadium concert," Fiona explained, "all of the kids in the audience—as well as the ones watching at home—will have to purchase these."

She held up a pair of headphones that looked as if they'd had a run in with a cat.

Official Josie and the Pussycats headphones.

Agent Kelly passed out headphone ears to all the other agents. Some tried them on, curious.

"Oooh, those look great on you," Fiona purred to one of the agents. But she made a face at another guy. "You—not so much." The man instantly swept them from his head.

Fiona walked around the room, so pumped over her latest power play. "But these are not just cute souvenirs, gentlemen. This is the debut of '3-D-X Surround Sound.' A new technology that makes the music feel like it's all around you. Like 3-D!"

Agent Kelly laced his hands together and cleared his throat. "But isn't sound already 3-D? I mean, technically speaking, isn't that stereo?"

"Who asked you?" Fiona snapped.

Scowling, she yanked aside a curtain to reveal a bunch of teenagers milling around behind a two-way glass wall. She and the agents could see the kids, but the kids couldn't see them.

The teenagers looked surly and dangerous . . . except for the fact that they were all wearing those cute little Pussycat headphones.

These research subjects had come from all over the country. Fiona peered in to look more closely and shuddered—there was that particularly unstylish girl Wyatt had "borrowed" from the MegaRecords store in Riverdale.

Some of the agents stepped back, afraid.

"Don't worry," Fiona assured them. "It's shatterproof glass. They can't get out."

The mostly middle-aged agents looked relieved.

"Now," Fiona went on, "this is what those kids *think* they're hearing over those headsets. . . ."

She turned up a knob so that the agents could hear inside the room. The sound of the new Josie and the Pussycats song blasted from the room. The teenagers began to jerk and sway, dancing to the hot rocking sounds.

"And *this*," Fiona added with a devilish smile, "is what they're *really* hearing."

She turned another knob, careful of her nails, and stood back with a smug look on her face to watch the agents' reactions.

A familiar voice boomed with authority:

*"You will obey your parents! You will not stay out past eleven o'clock! You will not drive like maniacs. . . ."*

"Hey, that voice . . ." Agent Kelly rubbed his chin, thinking hard. "I *know* that voice."

Fiona nodded. "It's Mr. Moviefone." She

laughed. "It's amazing, kids'll do anything he says. He does all our subliminal tracks."

*"You will* not *shine laser pointers at movie screens!"* Mr. Moviefone droned on. *"You will* not *laugh uncontrollably over something that's not really that funny . . ."*

Behind the glass, one by one, the kids stopped dancing, and their eyes glazed over, as the words they couldn't consciously hear began to flood their brains. One by one the kids sat down, like well-behaved . . . zombies. They just sat there, staring into space, with their hands folded neatly in their laps.

The agents gasped and murmured their amazement. They were totally impressed.

Fiona felt so clever she almost hugged herself! "Putting out messages on all those CDs that we sold in stores was a good start. But now—with this live concert even—we can reach them all at once . . ." Her words came faster and higher now, her eyes glowed as her excitement grew. "After the concert we'll have them all in our sway, obeying my *every* command . . . *The time has come, gentlemen!*" she shouted in victory, totally lost in dreams of power.

Agent Kelly licked his lips and glanced sideways at the other agents. "Well, that seems a little . . . intense."

Fiona glared. "Life is intense." Then she stepped up close to Agent Kelly, smiling up into his eyes. "Besides," she purred, "who's to say that we couldn't brainwash all the nubile teenage girls into thinking forty-something men in government-issue suits are just totally hot?"

Agent Kelly pondered this possibility. Then he shook Fiona's hand. "Excellent work, Fiona! These kids will *never* know what hit them!"

Fiona smiled and turned away. "And neither will you . . ."

"I'm sorry, what was that?" Agent Kelly asked.

Fiona froze. "What?"

"You just said something," Agent Kelly said.

"No, I didn't."

"Yes, you did," Agent Kelly insisted. "I said, 'These kids will never know what hit them.' And you said, 'And neither will you.' "

Fiona pretended to look clueless. "I did?"

"We all heard you," another agent piped up.

"Oh. Well, sure," Fiona said, laughing. "I was starting to say, 'And neither will you guys.' " She pointed to the kids still sitting like zombies behind the glass. "You know. 'You guys' meaning the teenagers. I was just emphasizing your point."

Agent Kelly frowned, but nodded. "Oh . . . okay. Great. Thanks."

"Anytime." Fiona smiled at him and turned. "That was close," she muttered.

"Excuse me?"

Fiona closed her eyes. *Damn!* But when she turned back around, she was wearing her most dazzling smile. "I was about to say, 'That was close to being a real nice moment between the two of us.' Don't you think?" She winked flirtatiously.

Agent Kelly smiled back, embarrassed. "Uh . . . sure. I guess."

There was an awkward pause. The other men were just standing there, watching everything.

"What are you guys looking at?" Agent Kelly snapped. "Come on, let's get back to the Pentagon."

Fiona watched them go—casually covering her mouth with her hand to keep anything else from slipping out.

These FBI guys were her boy toys—she needed to keep them happy and on her side to pull off this brilliant plan and help her make all her dreams come true.

# 10

Josie was hurrying to get dressed for Fiona's party when there was a knock at her hotel room door.

"Who is it?"

Her favorite singing voice in the world sang out, "I'm the guy who brought the pizza, the kind that's good to . . . eatsa."

Josie cringed. *Oops.* How in the world could she have forgotten the "date" she made with Alan M. Even if it was just to hang out, she could use a reality check right now. She ran to door and opened it.

Alan M. stood there smiling at her, with his guitar and a box of pizza—like a singing telegram. "I'm so sorry. But we've got to go to this . . ." Josie stammered. *How can I make it sound not wonderfully exciting?* "This . . . record party thing, with like the head of the label or something. . . . I'm sorry, I just totally flaked . . ."

She finally stopped talking and looked at him.

Alan M. wasn't moving. In fact, he looked like the stopped image on a video. And he was staring . . .

At her?

He swayed a little, then said, "Whoa."

"What's the matter?" Josie cried.

"N-nothing. You look so . . ." He waved a hand in the air.

Josie's face flushed hot and she pulled at the dress. "You can't make fun of me! They sent this dress over. I didn't pick it out. But I cut off the sleeves and turned them into wristbands." She glanced up at him through her lashes. "It looks stupid, doesn't it?"

"No. I didn't—I've just never seen you . . . *wow.*"

Josie was totally confused. "Finish your sentences. Is that a good wow or a bad wow?"

Alan M. slowly began to come back to life, and he smiled at her. "It's a good wow. It's a very good wow."

Josie blushed some more, this time from pleasure, although she was still a little embarrassed. "Oh . . . Thanks."

Alan M. smiled and nodded. And just kept staring.

Josie had to look away. But then she remembered:

"Um, actually . . . would you mind?" Josie turned around, revealing a completely backless dress.

Alan M. nearly choked as he stared at her long naked back. "Mind what?"

"The chain?"

Alan M. frowned, then noticed that there was a thin chain that ran down from her neck to the small of her back. It looked like it needed to be hooked to something. "Oh—right."

His hands fumbled nervously as he reached for the chain, his hand grazing her warm skin.

Josie's eyes closed as she savored the delicious feel of Alan's hands on her skin. With her back to him, she couldn't see that his expression very closely matched hers. Didn't see his hands lingering.

"Alan M.?"

Alan M. snapped out of his daze and quickly removed his hands as Josie turned around to face him.

"All done," he said, flustered.

Confused, Josie looked up at him. Their eyes met for a moment.

Josie's heart pounded like Melody's drum.

Could she really be seeing what she thought she saw in his eyes? Or was she only seeing what she wanted to see?

"Josie—you ready?" Wyatt Frame pushed through the partially open door wearing a killer tux and looking like something out of the movies.

But his sharp eyes quickly took in the plot brewing here in Josie's hotel room. "Hey! The door was open. I hope I'm not interrupting anything." He glanced at Alan M. "Hey, Alan N., how's it hangin'?"

"Actually, it's—"

"What's with the initial, anyway?" Wyatt scoffed. "Didn't work for Sheila E.—and it's not working for you."

He brushed at his spotless tux label, then turned to Josie. "We should get going, Jose. You don't want to be late for the hottest, most exclusive party of the year!"

Josie cringed. *Thanks a lot, Wyatt.*

Biting her lip, she smiled at Alan M. and pointed to her TV. "There's free cable," she said apologetically before Wyatt pulled her toward the door.

"Um, Josie!"

Josie turned back. "Yeah?"

Alan M.—usually the cool, confident hunk—

106

smiled at her awkwardly. "I was thinking, um, do you wanna . . . do something tomorrow?"

"Okay."

"When?" he asked quickly.

"Uh . . . two?" Josie suggested.

But Wyatt intervened, checking notes on his Palm Pilot. "No can do. Taping for *E!*"

"One thirty?" Alan M. suggested.

"MTV," Wyatt said.

"Three?"

"MSNBC."

"Four?"

"Four fifteen."

"Why?"

"Why not?"

Alan M. grabbed it. "Four fifteen."

"*Sold* to the young man with no future!" Wyatt quipped. With that, he swept his arm around Josie's shoulders and pulled her toward the door. "Now, Josie. We have a limo waiting."

"Okay . . ." Josie said reluctantly. She took one last look at Alan M. as Wyatt whisked her away. She didn't care how glamorous this party turned out to be—she knew it couldn't compare with the evening she might have had back in her room with a hometown boy and a hot pizza.

As Josie walked down the hall toward the elevator, Wyatt couldn't resist popping his head back in the door. "Good night, Adam 12!"

"It's—"

Wyatt slammed the door.

Alan M. sat down on the couch and opened the box of pizza and clicked on cable. But he didn't grab a slice—or look at the TV.

He was too busy thinking about Josie in that dress.

# 11

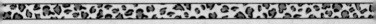

Meanwhile, down the hall, Melody was taking a shower before she got dressed for the party. The bathroom was so steamy, she could hardly see anything.

That's what she loved about nice hotels—lots and lots of hot water that never ran out. Not like at home, with three girls, one small bathroom, and a very stingy water heater.

Melody drew a great big smiley face on the steamy shower door, then added a happy little sun and a rainbow.

"If you're happy and you know it, clap your hands. . . ." Melody sang.

She clapped her hands—and dropped the soap.

Laughing, she picked it up again and continued singing.

"If you're happy and you know it, clap your

hands. . . ." She clapped again. And dropped the soap again.

Sing, clap, drop, stoop.

As she sang, and dropped, and picked up the soap through the entire song, she didn't notice the dark figure that entered her room. That crept closer and closer to the steamy bathroom. That slowly slipped in through the halfway open door.

Melody kept singing, oblivious to the figure's presence, and closed her eyes as she shampooed and rinsed her hair.

After a quick scrub with a body puff, she reached over and turned off the water.

Then opened the shower door—

And gasped in horror!

There, written in large letters in the steamy bathroom mirror, was a message—a terrifying message:

YOUR LIVES ARE IN DANGER.
BEWARE OF THE MUSIC.

Melody wrapped a plush towel around her body, then slowly approached the mirror, staring at the words, frightened.

Where had the words come from? Who had put them there?

Then she pulled herself together. She knew what to do.

She reached out toward the message and drew a happy face to dot the first i. Then she added a heart and a star over the second and third.

Then she heaved a great big sigh and smiled. "That's better."

Down the hall in her own room, Valerie was experiencing another kind of horror. She was putting on makeup while watching an episode of *Behind the Music*—the television show dedicated to dredging up the lives of celebrities whose music careers had long since crashed and burned.

She'd mostly turned on the tube for company. Valerie was used to sharing a place with Josie and Melody. She didn't understand why they all had to get separate rooms here at the hotel. These rooms were almost as big as their whole house back home. Valerie looked around. There was plenty of room for three friends to share.

But Wyatt had booked the rooms. He'd insisted that each girl deserved the luxury of their own space. After all, they were the hot new stars of American music. They could afford anything now.

Maybe. But why had Josie been so quick to agree to the arrangement? Val would have been happier with some roommates.

*"Not many people know that The Captain and Tennille got their start as a trio,"* the narrator on TV was saying. *Eddie 'Chief' Jones was their bassist."*

The camera zoomed in for a closeup of "Chief" Jones, sitting in a nice plush chair with a potted plant behind him. *"It's true,"* he said. *"Toni Tennille and I wrote all the songs together. The Captain just played the piano."*

"Yeah, right," Val muttered. *Another loser trying to ride the coattails of successful stars. I wonder if we'll have a lot of people trying to take advantage of our fame.*

Val glanced away from the mirror at the TV screen. An old stock photo showed a young Toni Tennille playing guitar next to a dark young man wearing a huge feathered headdress and playing bass guitar—the same instrument Valerie played.

*Must be the Chief,* Val thought and chuckled. *Hey, he can't be all bad if he plays the bass.*

Way off in the background, she could barely make out the tiny figure of The Captain sitting behind the piano.

"*It was even my idea to have him wear that hat,*" the Chief continued. "*I said, 'How're they gonna know you're the Captain if you don't wear a hat?'*"

Val watched, eye pencil in hand, and her eyes narrowed as she listened to what the Chief had to say.

"*Guess after a while they just didn't wanna share the spotlight anymore,*" the Chief complained. "*I mean, it's not like I'm that cat that got kicked outta Hall and Oates . . . But still, it's never fun to be left behind.*" The Chief shook his head. "*The Captain always said, 'Friends first and a band second.'*" He choked out a laugh, but bitter tears welled in his huge brown eyes. "*Wish I had that in writing.*"

Val nearly choked. That was exactly what Josie had said. In the beginning . . .

"Coming up—" the narrator broke in, "love *won't* keep them together. The Captain and Tennille hit the big time—*without* the Chief."

SNAP! Val looked down. She'd snapped her eye pencil in half.

# 12

Josie and her friends stood on the grand front porch of Fiona's mansion feeling like complete posers.

Josie gulped. *How'd I get here?* Part of her felt like bolting, back to the bowling alleys and pizza parlors of Riverdale. Back where she knew who she was and how to act and what to say.

Then she felt Wyatt's hand at the small of her back, giving her a gentle push forward.

*I guess there's no going back*, Josie thought. And for a moment, she wasn't sure why, she thought of Du Jour, had this strange feeling that they were looking down on her somehow. *Carpe diem*, Josie thought. *Time to seize your dreams*. With renewed confidence, she led the girls through the front door.

And Josie's confidence nose-dived like Du

Jour's plane. The Pussycats gaped. They'd never seen anything so spectacular in their lives, except on TV and in the movies. A full orchestra played as the huge room swarmed with hundreds of celebrities, models, and other beautiful and important people, laughing, talking, impressing one another with their own glamour and significance. Food and champagne flowed like there was no tomorrow.

Josie timidly led the girls a few steps into the room.

And everything stopped.

A hush fell over the crowd as all eyes focused on Josie and the Pussycats.

*Look at them staring at us*, Josie thought, horrified. *No one thinks I should be here. That's totally what they're thinking. . . .*

*Look at them staring at Josie*, Val thought. *No one thinks I should be here. That's totally what they're thinking. . . .*

Beside them, Melody mused, *If you're happy and you know it and you really want to show it, if you're happy and you know it, clap your hands . . .* And then she clapped her hands.

The moment she did, the lights dimmed.

*Did I do that?* Melody stuck her hands behind her back and wondered if this mansion had a Clapper.

But no one was looking at Melody, or any of

the Pussycats, now. They'd turned toward the grand staircase that led to the huge foyer. The orchestra played a fanfare. A dozen handsome men dressed in sleek tuxedoes dashed forward and took their places along the railings lining the stairs. As they held out their hats and canes, aiming toward the top of the stairs, a spotlight clicked on.

And into that dazzling circle of light stepped . . .

Fiona.

Two of the tuxedoed men leaned in a choreographed arch just long enough to take photographs of the great beauty in her fairytale gown.

"My god, she's fabulous!" Wyatt exclaimed from his planted position in the middle of the crowd. And everyone around him agreed.

After posing for a few moments, so everyone could admire her gown completely, Fiona began to descend the stairs, in time to the music. When she reached the second landing, another tuxedoed dancer climbed out from under the landing to hand Fiona a crystal glass of champagne.

Fiona took a single sip and handed it back.

The crowd *ooohed*.

"I've never seen anyone so magnificent!" This time Wyatt's exclamation came from another well-placed spot in the crowd on the other side of the room. The people were instantly inspired by his expression of admiration and began to call out their own—as Wyatt raced to another section of the room.

As Fiona came down the last third of the stairs, two more dancers rushed out to greet her and dashed up the stairs, taking with them a piece of fabric trailing from her dress. Fiona spun awkwardly as they ran, unraveling her gown, till—ta-da!—they revealed her bustier costume underneath.

It was totally bizarre. And the crowd totally ate it up.

"I feel like a child on Christmas morning!" Wyatt shouted from the far side of the room. He clapped wildly, and the primed crowd burst into applause.

Fiona smiled, greeting her audience, soaking up the admiration just long enough so as not to ruin the effect. Then she turned her gaze outward, searching the crowd.

"Now, where are my guests of honor?"

Uh-oh—that's us! Josie didn't know if she could bear to stand next to this woman in the spotlight. She might just melt from the glare.

But then Fiona saw her. It was too late to duck under a table. Josie braced herself for the attention. "There are my girls!" she cried, pointing them out to the crowd. "MegaRecords' newest recording sensations, everybody! And aren't they just divine?"

The crowd parted like the Red Sea before Moses as she swept across the room toward Josie. Josie stuck out her hand for a handshake, but Fiona ignored it and enveloped each one in a showy hug, followed by a triple Euro air kiss.

"I'm Fiona," she said—unnecessarily. "Welcome to your party!"

Watching like an audience at the theater, the crowd burst into cheers.

Fiona basked in the moment, sharing the attention with the Pussycats, then leaned in to Josie.

"Enough spectacle," she whispered as if they were the best of girlfriends. "Let's go be girls."

Fiona giggled as she shut the door to her bedroom—her very, very pink bedroom. "This is my girly room," she confided. "No boys allowed."

Val and Josie looked around, appalled at the unexpected décor. The rest of Fiona's home was like something out of *House Beautiful*—sophisticated, elegant, luxurious.

But this room—it looked like the bedroom of a spoiled little cupcake of a girl. The bed overflowed with dozens and dozens of stuffed animals. A huge, elaborate Victorian dollhouse stood in the corner. The bed and canopy looked like a pink birthday cake with all its frills and lace. And everything—the walls, the carpet, the bedding, the chairs—were pink, pink, pink.

"Come, sit down," Fiona said. "We'll gossip."

A uniformed houseboy entered with a huge silver tray overflowing with cookies, junk food, and champagne.

"Just leave it right here, Gregor," Fiona instructed him.

As soon as he left, Fiona leaned toward Josie. "Tell me he's not just the cutest!"

"He's pretty cute. . . ." Josie said politely.

Fiona giggled. "Wouldn't you just love to strip him down and roll him in cookie dough?"

Josie's mouth fell open. She and her friends exchanged a look. *Uh . . . what's going on here?*

But just then Melody spotted one of her favorite foods on the silver tray. "Ooh, Doritos!"

"Mmm! Yes!" Fiona exclaimed. "Let's just pig out!"

The Pussycats each took a plate and piled it high with junk food, then sat back down on the plush pink carpet. But then they watched, confused, as Fiona delicately placed food on her plate—one Dorito, a cheese curl, and five carefully counted M&M's. Then she flopped down on the carpet next to Josie and began to massage her.

Josie jumped to her feet. "What are you doing?"

"Massage chain!" Fiona giggled. "Come on, it'll be just like a slumber party!"

Reluctantly Josie sat down and joined the weird massage chain. She'd seen a lot of strange things in the music business, but this was pretty bizarre. She looked around for all the exits.

"So, Josie," Fiona asked. "What do you weigh?"

"What?"

"Your weight," Fiona asked in a conspiratorial whisper.

Josie sighed. "One . . . eighteen."

"Hah!" Fiona crowed. "One fifteen! I'm three pounds lighter than you!" she bragged gleefully.

Josie looked at the Twinkie in her hand.

"Oh, no!" Fiona cried. "Keep eating! Don't worry about it. I think you look great!"

Josie shrugged. She devoured the Twinkie in two bites and licked her fingers. It tasted so sugary sweet good that she reached for another one.

Fiona glared down at her lone Dorito as if she wanted to smash it to bits. "Tho pretty and popular."

Josie frowned and leaned forward. "What'd you say?"

Fiona swallowed. *Caught again.* "Nothing." She cleared her throat. "I said, 'The new thong's pretty popular.' "

Valerie made a face. "What thong?"

"I don't like thongs," Melody said. "It's like a constant wedgie."

"No, I meant thong!" Fiona insisted. "The new thingle!"

The girls had no idea what she was talking about. And what was up with that weird lisp all of a sudden?

Fiona turned away, embarrassed. "Excuthe me," she said quietly. "I mutht have thome food caught in my teeth." Awkwardly she scrambled up from the floor and dashed behind a translucent pink screen. Josie and Val and Mel could see her in silhouette.

And they could hear her as she began to talk to herself, as if she were alone in the room.

"Thtop it! Thtop it thith thecond!" Slap!

The Pussycats watched in slack-jawed silence. The woman had actually slapped herself!

"You're tho pathetic! You loother!" And then the woman slapped herself again!

A few seconds later, she stepped out from behind the screen, adjusting her hair, poised and composed once more.

The girls stared at her, their mouths hanging open.

Fiona smiled like a beauty queen. "Got it," she said, referring to the food between her teeth. "Hey, who wants to French braid?"

Josie took a step toward the door, and glanced at Val. *What the hell is going on?* It was like Dr. Jekyll and Ms. Hyde. The woman they were seeing now was like the total opposite of the sophisticated but outrageous woman who had wowed the crowd downstairs just moments before.

Fiona must have realized her guests were getting a bit squirmy, and that her little girl talk slumber party was a total bomb. But the next thing she said was, "Oh, look at me, hoarding you girls away in here. You should be out enjoying your party. Meeting people! I want everyone everywhere to be talking about you! Go on. . . ."

With a dramatic gesture she flung open the door for them.

The girls didn't have to be invited twice. "Head for the exit," Josie whispered to Val, "and don't look back."

The girls hurried down a back staircase and slipped out into the gardens. But even here they couldn't escape the excesses of their strange host—and the woman who, as head of MegaRecords, held their music career in the palm of her hand.

123

Here in the center of an elaborate patio garden rose a huge lighted ice sculpture garden. The giant letters F I O N A arranged in a glorious semicircle sparkled under the lights.

"Okay," said Valerie. "Who else thinks Fiona's a freak?"

"Oh, my god," Melody exclaimed. "I'm so glad you said something, because as soon as you said her name, I got the most awful sensation. Like an ice-cold chill creeping up my spine!"

Valerie looked at Melody: "That's because you're sitting on the O."

Melody glanced down. She was indeed sitting on a big ice sculpture O. "Oh." She leaped up and stepped down.

She stopped, considered a moment, then shook her head. "No, I'm still feeling the shivers. And it's not the O. It's her."

Josie sighed. "Yeah, you could be right. She did seem a little loopy. I mean, she only ate one Dorito."

"You know what else is loopy?" Melody said. "Those girls from Riverdale. How come they're here? And how come they're not throwing things at me?"

Val nodded in agreement. "Yeah, it was like . . . they were zombies or something."

Melody whirled around, clutching her

124

friends' arms. "Oh, my god. What if somebody brainwashed them into liking us, and we're actually just pawns in some great big conspiracy involving advertising, the government, and the media?"

The girls thought about this for a moment.

But then Melody's tinkling laughter distracted them. "Oh, my god! Look! That basset hound's made entirely out of ice! That's so funny!" She ran over to admire it, her earlier worries completely forgotten.

But Josie was deep in thought. "What do you think, Val?"

Valerie sighed, like she didn't want to think about it. "Well, stuff's definitely been . . . different since we left Riverdale." She peered at Josie, then decided to say something she'd been wanting to say for a while. "And if you ask me, some things feel like they've changed completely."

But Josie wasn't listening, which Valerie took as just one more confirmation that Josie was beginning to ignore her friends, and leave them behind. Valerie strode off to look at the ice cube basset hound with Melody. At least Melody was still her friend.

Valerie couldn't hear what was really in Josie's mind. Still deep in thought, Josie gazed at Fiona's mansion, glowing with party lights, illuminating the rich and famous. It was the kind of fiesta she'd often dreamed of being invited to, but now . . . well, she seemed to have lost her appetite for it.

Upstairs in the mansion, curled up in her pink bedroom, Fiona stared at her security monitor, watching the Pussycats' entire conversation. She leaned back in her pink silk down-stuffed chair, munching M&M's that matched her outfit . . . M by M.

"Wyatt," she complained, "why is it that celebrities have this unyielding desire to also be smart? I mean, they get the adulation of millions, free clothes, their picture on the cover of *In Style* magazine. *And* yet it's just not enough. 'Look at me'," she mocked in a high whiny voice. " 'I'm not just pretty, I have a brain! Put me on *Politically Incorrect*!' " Fiona scowled. "Like anybody cares."

She glared at the monitor, then whirled to face Wyatt. "For god's sake, isn't being famous enough? Just smile and sit quietly, and leave the thinking to the masterminds. Like me."

"Indeed," Wyatt said wisely.

Fiona punched a pink pillow. "I don't like those two Pussycats. They're asking questions, and that's dangerous. We can't afford to take any more risks."

"I'll get rid of them," Wyatt assured her quickly. "Find you a new band by the morning."

He winced as Fiona beaned him with an M&M.

"Think, Wyatt! We've already sold half a million Josie ears for the Big Concert!"

"Right," Wyatt said. He rubbed his head, amazed that a tiny candy-coated chocolate could hurt like that. "So . . . what are you suggesting?"

Fiona sat up, all traces of any lisp gone now as she was once again in charge. "Keep Josie," she told Wyatt. "And put those two nosy Pussycats to sleep."

Wyatt hesitated to disagree, but he'd gotten to know Josie a little. "Josie'll never play without her friends."

Fiona smiled deviously. "Oh, I think we might persuade her." She set down her bowl of M&M's and stared at the blank TV in her room, as if picturing a news bulletin. "Next," Fiona said, imitating a newscaster, "on *Behind the Music*, Josie suffers a tragic loss. . . ."

# 13

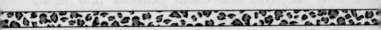

Josie had always dreamed of shopping at FAO Schwartz, the most fabulous toy store in the world.

But this was even better. The store was packed—with people who came just to see the Pussycats.

Josie sat at a long fancy table signing boxes of the new Josie and the Pussycat dolls.

Val and Melody shared a tiny table off to the side, sitting on folding metal chairs.

Valerie scowled, grinding her fist in her hand. The lines in front of Josie's table were long—literally hundreds clutching Josie dolls queued up to get their doll boxes signed, to have their picture taken with Josie, to touch her, to gush how much they loved her, to breathe the same air as her. To share her germs. . . .

*Doesn't anybody want our germs?* Valerie grumbled.

The lines weren't so long for Val and Mel. Like, there was nobody in them.

Beside her, Melody giggled and Val looked to see what she could possibly find funny about this situation.

*I can't believe it!* Valerie thought. Melody was playing with a Josie doll.

"Look!" Melody exclaimed. "Josie's doing yoga!" She twisted the flexible doll into a complicated position.

Val looked at her own doll. "My doll's knees don't even bend." Furious, she tried to make one bend—and the whole leg broke right off. "I don't believe this!" Feeling as if she was losing control, she yanked her anger management book out of her back pocket, opened it to a random page, and tried to focus on the words. But all she could see was *Josie* and the pussycats. *Josie, Josie, Josie.*

*I always liked that name,* Valerie thought. *But now I'm starting to hate it very much.*

"All right," she said, deciding to be straight with Melody about her feelings. "Let me just ask you something. Have you noticed that everything has . . . sort of become all about Josie?"

"Um . . . no," Melody said softly.

*She's lying!* Valerie thought. *I can always tell. She gets this little crease on her forehead because she feels so bad when she fibs.*

Valerie wouldn't let it drop. "You swear on a litter of pugs you haven't even noticed one time?"

Melody looked as if she was about to burst into tears. "Why did you have to bring pugs into this?" she shouted. She crossed her arms and swore in her mind she'd never speak to Valerie again. "Yeah . . ." she said twenty seconds later. "Of course I noticed. But I felt really bad for thinking it, so I stopped."

Valerie laid a hand on Melody's shoulder. "Well, if we're both feeling this way, I think we need to say something to Josie."

Melody's conflicted emotions showed plainly on her face. "I'm sure she's not doing anything on purpose, Val. Maybe we're just feeling kind of weird because of the new band name."

"The band's equal parts the three of us," Val insisted hotly. "Why should she get all the attention?" She stared at her one-legged Valerie doll. "And articulated limbs?"

Melody thought about that. She stared over at the long line of people waiting eagerly to meet Josie.

Josie looked up from signing a box at just

that moment and waved, a friendly smile on her face.

"That bitch!" Melody blurted. "She's totally trying to shove us out of the way and steal the spotlight for herself!"

With a horrified gasp, Melody covered her mouth with both hands, her eyes wide in disbelief. "Oh, my god! Did I just say that? I promise, I didn't mean it, Val." She gazed back at Josie, with a guilty look on her face, as if somehow Josie would know she'd said it.

"Maybe we're overacting," Melody said to convince herself. "We should just give it a few days, right? I mean, people still care about us."

Just then a kid's father rushed up to Valerie's table.

*See?* Melody's expression said.

Val smiled up at the man, her pen raised, ready to sign her first autograph. Then she noticed he wasn't holding a box.

Suddenly the man grabbed the one-legged Valerie doll out of Valerie's hand, dropped to his knees, raised the doll overhead, then smashed it over and over and over again on the floor.

Val stood up, a horrified scream stuck in her throat.

The man caught his breath, then casually tossed the beaten, busted doll back to Valerie.

She held it up. It was totally headless now, twisted irreparably.

"Sorry," the man apologized. "There was a spider crawling toward Josie's table."

Val gripped the mutilated doll in her hand and began to chant, "Shoving this where the sun don't shine will not make me feel better."

Melody leaned over and patted Valerie's hand. "It might."

# 14

That afternoon, at exactly four-fifteen, after dozens of interviews and appearances, Josie kept her date with Alan M.

But they couldn't just walk down the city streets anymore. Too many people recognized Josie and insisted on taking just a teeny tiny piece of her time.

But Josie had an idea. A place where they could escape to another world, of peaceful deep blues and greens.

The Aquarium.

Even as a child, Josie had always loved aquariums, loved to watch the fish and sea mammals swim freely in the underwater worlds. Of course, it was an illusion, because they were actually in cages, and not free at all. But maybe it was the illusion that mattered. Did the seals and whales and sharks feel free?

Or did they know they were swimming in cages?

She attempted not to think of how that metaphor applied to her music and her deal with MegaRecords.

Instead, she tried to forget it all, and simply immerse herself in a few quiet moments with Alan M.

They'd looked at the sea mammals and the tiger sharks. They'd made faces at some of the ugly fish. And they'd even picked up starfish and petted a stingray in the hands-on exhibit.

Now they just strolled down the stairs in comfortable silence. Josie enjoyed watching the group of noisy schoolchildren clustered around the glass of a huge tank, squirming and gasping out things like "Cool!" and "Oh, wow!" as their teacher tried to make them pay attention to the tour guide with a microphone who was lecturing them about sturgeons.

"You know I'm playing a gig tonight," Alan M. said suddenly.

"You are?" Josie exclaimed. "That's great!" She searched his face, wondering why he hadn't told her.

But the look in his eyes, in his body language, told her. He was thinking it wasn't very important compared to Josie's outrageous career.

"Yeah. It's just this bar," he said, shrugging, "but I played the manager my demo, and he said I could have an hour tonight. You think . . ." He seemed almost afraid to ask. "Maybe you'd wanna come?"

Would she? How could he think she wouldn't? "Yeah! Of course!"

Alan M. shrugged again, rubbing a stain on the carpet with the toe of his shoe. "Cause I know you've been busy and all. . . ."

"Oh, but Alan M.—"

That was as far as she got before the screams ripped through the aquarium.

"Oh, my god!" they heard the tour guide shriek through her microphone so that everyone on the entire floor could hear. "It's *Josie*!"

Josie froze. She still wasn't used to this. *Will I ever be?* she wondered.

The school kids turned and spotted her. And suddenly a whole pack of eight- and nine-year olds were screaming and chasing her like a pack of hungry wolves on a nature show.

Alan M. grabbed Josie and ran, down a ramp, past a door marked KEEP OUT. Then he skidded to a stop and yanked her inside with him.

Seconds after they closed the door, they heard the kids stampede by them.

Holding hands, Josie and Alan looked

around. They were in a quiet darkened room. In the huge blue tank behind them, graceful Beluga whales swam like giant ballerinas.

Josie caught her breath and smiled up at Alan M. "Thanks."

"No problem."

Josie stared at a passing whale for a moment as it seemed to sail effortlessly through its silent world. Something deep down inside of her yearned for a place like that.

"How am I gonna pull this off?" she murmured.

"What?" Alan M. asked softly.

Josie shook her head and sighed. "I'm just a girl from Riverdale. I'm not a rock star."

Alan M. stepped closer and smiled down into her eyes. "Oh, Josie, you've been waiting your whole life for this."

"I know. I'm just . . . I'm scared."

"Don't be," he told her. "You have to believe in yourself."

"What if I can't?"

"Then I'll believe in you for you."

Josie smiled and felt as if she were sailing through peaceful silent blue waters.

She swayed toward him. He took her into his arms . . .

Thunk! Thunk! Thunk!

Josie and Alan M. looked over at the tank.

Unbelievable! A tourist in a wet suit and air tank was swimming with the whales. But instead of photographing the giant mammals with his underwater camera, he waved and snapped a picture of Josie.

Josie groaned. The moment was definitely ruined. Awkwardly she and Alan M. headed for the exit.

Wyatt would be waiting for her. She had an appointment she had to get back for, but for the life of her she couldn't remember what could possibly be so important.

"What do you think we should do for the concert?" Josie asked the other Pussycats that night before dinner. They'd just come in from swimming in the hotel pool, and for once they were hanging out in Josie's room, just like old times. "Should we open with 'Three Small Words' or 'Come On'?"

"I don't know," Valerie said distractedly. She was staring at the cover of the magazine Melody was reading. It was the latest issue of *Vanity Fair*, and it had Josie on the cover, body-painted with leopard spots. Alone.

*When did she do that shoot?* Valerie wondered.

Josie picked up her acoustic guitar and strummed a few lines from a new song she was working on. "I mean, we could try 'Roll on Rollie Wheel.' But I still think the lyrics need work."

Val started to answer, but then she noticed the Coke can Melody was drinking from: It was a Josie can.

*When did we get Coke cans?* Valerie wondered.

"Val, what do you think?" Josie pressed.

Val sighed and stared out the window at the colors of a sunset streaking the sky. But wait—something was floating by the window. Something huge. She got up and walked to the window for a better look. And what she saw moving slowly across the sky blew her away:

A leopard-painted blimp, with an enormous Josie head smiling above the words: LOG ON TO JOSIE.COM!

Valerie slumped down in her chair, grinding her teeth. "It's your call, Josie. You're the boss."

Josie put down her guitar. "No, I'm not. What's up with you?"

Val stared at her best friend—or rather, the girl who used to be her best friend. Was she so totally clueless? Or was the innocent act a part of her game?

*We gotta talk this out,* Valerie told herself. That's what her anger management book told her to do, anyway. She opened her mouth to bring it up.

But then Wyatt walked into the room.

"Hello, girls! How are the most beautiful and talented women in rock and roll?"

"Don't you mean 'woman'?" Val said pointedly.

"Valerie, dear," Wyatt replied smoothly, "you must learn to take a compliment. What are you going to do when you go on *TRL* tonight and Carson Daly tells you how much he loves your music?"

Total Request Live? Valerie's heart skipped a beat. She loved that show! But then her heart sank. It wasn't her they were after. "You mean, what's *Josie* going to do?"

Wyatt tried not to smile as he tossed out his bait. "She won't be there. We just booked you and Melody."

Valerie's head whipped up in surprise.

"Um-hmm," Wyatt confirmed. "It's time for the world to get to know the *other* Pussycats."

"We're going on *TRL*?!" Melody gushed. "Do I get to touch Carson?!"

Wyatt grinned. He was pretty sure he'd just bagged himself two troublesome Pussycats. "Anywhere you like. The taping starts in two hours." Then he sobered: "Unless you've got a problem with this."

Valerie definitely did not. But she turned to Josie. "Have *you* got a problem with this?"

"Me?" Josie shook her head. "Of course not.

141

You guys'll have so much fun! I love that show."

"And you don't feel bad that we're going on without you?" Valerie wanted to make sure.

"Why? I don't care about that stuff."

Valerie felt all her anger melting away. She smiled at Josie and gave her a big hug. "I'm so sorry, Jose. I don't know what I was thinking."

Since Josie had no idea what Val *had* been thinking, she was a little confused by Val's outburst. "Okay."

"Come on, ladies," Wyatt said, shattering the friend fest. He was trying to break up the band, not get them back together. "We've got stylists and designers waiting in your rooms."

Val and Melody looked at each other and squealed in excitement, then ran down the hotel hallway to their suites.

When the girls were gone, Wyatt sat down next to Josie. "And *you* have homework tonight," he announced. He reached inside his jacket and pulled out an unlabeled CD. "This is a remix of your next single—the ballad? I'm curious to get your thoughts." He waved the CD at her.

Josie groaned like a high school kid who'd been grounded. "Can it wait till tomorrow, Wyatt? It's just that Alan M.'s playing his first gig tonight, and I want to get there early."

Wyatt simmered. *Alan Alphabet again.* He was getting pretty tired of that unemployed folksinger hanging around all the time. He didn't like the vibes he picked up between the loser and Josie. Anything developing in the romance department between those two would definitely get in the way of his management of this little project.

*Time to nip this romance in the bud,* he decided. Then he'd see about buying country boy a bus ticket home. But Josie was smarter than most of the teen heartthrobs he'd dealt with in the past. He'd have to be careful.

"Ohh. I'm so sorry, Josie. I forgot to tell you. Alan M. called my office earlier. They canceled his show."

"They did? Why didn't he call me here?"

"Um—" Good question. What was a good answer? "He probably did. I'm sure, when you go down to the front desk, there will be a message waiting. Excuse me."

Wyatt got to his feet, pulled out his cell phone, and walked a few steps away so he could whisper into the phone without Josie hearing him.

Josie watched him curiously.

Wyatt flipped his phone closed and rejoined her, nodding. "Yes. The message is down there waiting for you. Now."

Josie sighed. "Well, I guess I should call him."

"Oh, you can't!" *Why?* "Because . . . he also said to tell you that he wouldn't be reachable for a few hours, but he'll call you as soon as he can."

Josie looked incredulous. "All that was on the message downstairs?"

A muscle jumped in Wyatt's jaw. "Okay. Yes. Excuse me." He walked a few steps away and placed another whispery call.

Then he turned back to Josie. "Yes. That's *all* on the message. Anything else?" He held up his cell phone, prepared to make another quick call.

"Who do you keep calling?"

Wyatt's face hardened. *Time to try a different approach here.* "I'm running a label here, Josephine. And I have other artists who need me and need my time. Other artists who aren't quite so difficult about doing a little extra work." He dangled the CD in front of her nose again. "Frankly, your level of non-commitment makes me question your commitment. So you want to be a rock superstar, live large, big house, five cars?" Josie stared at him with a puzzled look. "You have to do the time. Or someone else will. And then *you'll* be left to explain it to Val and Mel."

Wyatt's final words hit home. Josie looked *very* guilty. "I-I'm sorry, Wyatt."

Wyatt shrugged as if not convinced.

"I *am* committed," Josie insisted.

Wyatt suppressed a grin and thrust the CD at her.

This time Josie took it. "I *am*," she said with determination.

Wyatt beamed. "I know, love. I know."

# 15

Valerie and Melody held hands as they entered the dark studio.

"Val!" Melody whispered. "We're on *TRL*!"

Excited, they slapped each other a major high five.

But where was everybody? As they ventured farther into the studio, Valerie noticed something surprising. "Check out the view." She went to the window that looked over Times Square—and stuck her hand right through an empty frame. "It's . . . fake!" There was not even any glass in the window, and the view behind it was simply a photograph.

"Wow, this stuff looks *so* different on TV!" Melody said. She reached out to touch the flatscreen monitor. The letters TRL were spelled out with masking tape! Melody tugged at the tape, and the whole monitor broke off! It was made of cheap cardboard.

Both girls turned around slowly, studying the set. That's when they noticed that the entire *audience* was filled with cardboard people.

"Uh-oh. Val?" Melody was getting spooked.

"This isn't right," Valerie said, looking around. "I mean, where is everybody? Where's Carson?"

"Right over here, ladies."

The girls whirled around to see a figure emerge from behind the seats. Melody quickly hid the fake monitor behind her back. She didn't want to start off on the wrong foot with Mr. Daly.

But the figure who stepped into the light wasn't Carson Daly. It was the actor Jack Black. Val and Mel had seen him in *Hi Fidelity* and Jack looked nothing like Carson.

"Hey, what's up? I'm Carson Daly. Thanks for coming to the show."

Val stared in disbelief. "You're not Carson Daly."

"Sure I am," Jack Black replied.

"I told you things look different on TV," Melody whispered.

"The camera takes off ten pounds," Jack Black explained. "You should see what Al Roker looks like in person." He puffed out his cheeks and posed like a sumo wrestler.

"Wait a minute," Valerie said. "The camera *adds* ten pounds."

"It does?" Jack Black looked down at himself as he took in that info. "Oh, jeez. That's not good."

Valerie had had enough of this ridiculous joke. "Okay, this isn't *TRL* and you're not Carson. We're outta here." She headed toward the door, pulling a very confused Melody behind her.

The real Carson Daly stepped out of the shadows and blocked their way.

"Aw, don't leave, Pussycats. We haven't even started the show."

"Oh, my god!" Melody screamed. "It's Carson!"

"Oh, my god!" Carson squealed, mocking Melody's voice. "It's Melody!"

Valerie shook her head to clear it. "Okay, wait. So this is *TRL*?"

Carson folded his arms and pretended to ponder the question. "Well, it's not quite *Total Request Live*. You could say it's more like: *Total Request . . . Dead*."

Suddenly his eyes sparkled wickedly. He pulled two baseball bats from behind his back and tossed one to Jack Black.

"Yeah, see we received only one request to-day. . . ." Jack said. He started twirling the bat menacingly.

The girls turned back to Carson.

"And that's to kill you," Carson announced.

He raised his bat, looked at Jack, and then they both laughed.

Relieved, the girls started laughing, too. See? Valerie thought. They're kidding. This was all some kind of weird practical joke. Who set it up? Valerie wondered. Josie? Wyatt? Or was it both of them?

But just as the girls relaxed, Carson and Jack stopped laughing. The expressions on their faces were cold and dead serious.

Valerie's laughter died in her throat.

But Melody kept laughing. "That was so funny! Carson said he was going to kill us. Like that was the request. . . ."

"He's not kidding," Val told her.

Melody looked at the celebrity in disbelief.

Carson shook his head and shrugged. Sorry.

Then Carson and Jack rushed toward them with bat raised.

Melody and Val screamed.

# 16

Josie turned off the tap and stepped into the huge hotel bathtub. It should have felt wonderful as she sank down into the hot water and bubbles. It should have been a welcome break from the crazy schedule she'd had this week. And it should have felt luxurious to have a bathroom all to herself, without Mel running in and out every five seconds to get something she forgot, without Val pounding on the door shouting, "Hurry up—and save some hot water for the rest of us!"

But for some reason, Josie felt a little blue. Like she was missing all the fun.

She should have been sitting in some cozy little bar listening to Alan M. sing his sweet songs as if they were meant only for her to hear. And she couldn't help but wish she were off with Valerie and Melody, at the *TRL* taping. *Bet they're having a blast,* she thought miserably.

Maybe it was just her turn to feel blue. Reluctantly, she popped Wyatt's CD into the Discman, slipped on the headphones, and pressed Play.

The music would make her feel better. It always did.

She settled back and closed her eyes to listen.

It was a recording of the Pussycats singing a sweet ballad. She listened a minute, then shook her head. Yes, it was them, her words, and music. But something had happened to their simple honest song when it went through MegaRecords' machines. She couldn't quite put her finger on it. But somehow they'd managed to make a ballad come out sounding like an overproduced pop song.

The phone rang, but Josie didn't hear it through the headphones and music.

The phone rang and rang and rang . . . over and over, way beyond the number of rings most people would wait through. It might have been important.

Josie's eyes glazed over as the sounds of the CD wormed their way into her brain. . . .

Halfway across town from the luxury hotel, in a seedy bar in an iffy neighborhood, Alan M. stood at the pay phone, listening to it ring.

Josie had said she was coming tonight.

*Guess something came up.*

Finally he gave up. He did have a gig to perform—even if it wasn't as important as Josie's.

He walked a few steps and sat down on a stool between the phone, the exit, the pool table, and the men's room. This was Alan M.'s stage. He didn't mind the *whoosh* and *crack!* of the pool games so much. But the flushing and ringing kind of interrupted his songs.

Maybe it would be best if Josie didn't show up after all.

"Well, this next song is dedicated to a . . . friend of mine. I kind of wanted to wait till she showed up to play it, but I guess she . . ."

His words faded away as he looked at the small table he'd saved for Josie right by the stage. It was tiny, and he'd had to stuff a wadded-up napkin under one leg to keep it from wobbling. But he'd placed a RESERVED sign on the table, and even set a single rose in a vase in the center.

"Whoop! Hoodoo!"

Alan cringed. Of course Alexandra was there. She was dressed in a very skimpy outfit, sitting as close to the stage as she could get. She was even holding a homemade banner that read I'M WITH THE BAND!

153

"Well, anyway," Alan M. started out. "It's called 'Wish You Felt the Same.' "

He blew into the harmonica, strummed the guitar . . .

And a loud flush rang out from the toilet . . .

Alexandra bellowed *Shut up or hold it till you get home!* Then she turned and smiled sweetly, waiting for Alan M. to play.

*Smash!*

Valerie screamed!

Jack Black aimed for Valerie's head, but destroyed a fake camera instead.

"C'mon baby . . ." Jack sang as he swung the bat, "Don't fear the Reaper . . . Just take my hand . . ." He backed her into a corner, and Valerie threw one of the flat screens at him, but he easily knocked it away.

"No, really. 'Don't fear the Reaper . . . Naa, na, naaa, naaa, na . . .' "

At other end of stage, the real Carson Daly was backing Melody up into the audience bleachers.

"I can't believe you're a killer," Melody told him, nearly in tears. "You seem so nice on TV."

"Oh, yeah?" Carson snapped. "Well, try sixty-five days with 'Bye Bye Bye' in the top five. Try hundreds of high-pitched squealy voices crying out for Justin right in your ear. It's like shrapnel! Try acting like"—he made air quotes—"*Raymond* is your best pal when he constantly steals all the Oreos off the craft service table. Yeah, it's so *nice*! Do you have any idea how much rage I have built up inside me?!"

"Sorry I brought it up."

Carson swung at Melody's head, but she ducked out of the way just in time. As she crouched down, she searched the ground for something—anything!—to use as a weapon.

There—she quickly grabbed a cardboard cutout of Christina Aguilera—and whomped Carson in the gut.

"Ow!" Carson whined, seriously annoyed.

Melody took the chance to hit him over and over with Christina.

Carson blocked the blows with his hands, but dropped his bat, and watched it roll down the stairs.

"Okay. Fine." Carson grabbed the cutout of Britney Spears and swung at her. She blocked with Christina. They dueled.

Meanwhile Jack was still singing "Don't Fear the Reaper" as he made his moves on Val. When he reached the guitar solo, he threw his head back, playing air guitar, and Val took that opportunity to give him a roundhouse kick to the crotch.

Jack's eyes shot open and he glared at Val.

"*Not* during the guitar solo. God! That's just like a bass player."

Val slipped past him, but he spun around, fuming. "You don't mess with Blue Oyster Cult!"

He swung the bat over his head and howled like an animal. This time he ran full speed straight at Val.

Val looked around. She had made her way to the fake windows, but now there was nowhere to go. She turned around, backed up against the set, as Jack came barreling at her.

At the last second Val dived out of the way, and Jack went flying past—through the window, ripping through the city translight, and *Bam*! headfirst into the brick stage wall behind it.

He dropped to the ground, out cold.

Val looked up into the audience seats to see . . .

Mel and Carson dueling with the pop-star cutouts.

Mel ripped a nasty gash into Britney with Christina.

"Ha! Britney can't hold up to Christina!"

But Carson tossed Britney aside and pulled out . . . Mariah Carey!

"Uh-oh . . ." Melody whispered.

Carson swung Mariah and knocked

Christina's head clean off. Melody yelped and dropped her. Now Carson had her backed up against the railing at the top of the seats. Smiling devilishly, he prepared to strike the final blow.

"Wait! Wait! Wait!" Melody cried. "I have one question."

Carson paused. "It'll be your last."

"Okay. Is your name really Carson Daly? Or is that just because your show's on every day? You know, like Carson, comma, daily?"

Carson looked around, confused. "What? That's the stupidest question I've ever—"

As his head turned back to Melody, he saw Whitney Houston come flying at his face. *Wham!* Melody smashed him with the Whitney cutout, knocking him right over the railing. He screamed as he fell twenty feet to the stage floor.

Melody peered over the railing with her Whitney cutout. "Don't mess with the queen diva, baby."

Val came running up the stairs to Melody.

"So what was *that* all about?" Melody asked her.

"I have no idea," Valerie gasped. "Let's get out of here and find Josie!"

# 17

"Josie! *Josie!* Quick—open the door!"

Josie was in the bedroom of her hotel suite, posing and posturing in front of the mirror. She vaguely heard the knocking through the headphones she still wore, but she was too busy working on her look to bother. She pouted, smiled at herself, and struck big rock star stances—all to the sounds of the CD that Wyatt had told her to play.

But the pounding continued.

"Josie!" Valerie shouted through the door. "Quick! Open the door!"

In a huff, Josie yanked off her headphones and stalked over to the door. She peeked through the tiny little privacy peephole to see who was there.

"Oh, joy," she muttered, annoyed. "Little

Miss Goody Two-shoes and her friend, Polly-anna."

Josie flung open the door. "What."

Val and Melody rushed in, closing the door behind them.

"We've gotta talk to you!" Val gasped.

"How did you get up here?" Josie snapped. "I specifically told the front desk *no visitors*."

"Ha, ha," Valerie said. "Seriously, Jose, listen—"

Josie glared. "Did I tell you you could speak to me?"

Val stared at her, confused.

Melody looked worried. "Are you okay, Jose?"

"Why wouldn't I be okay? I have the number one single in the country." She scoffed. "You, on the other hand, should maybe be a little worried. . . ."

With that, Josie twirled on her heel and walked back to the mirror to put on more lip gloss.

Val and Melody exchanged looks. This was even weirder than the scene at *TRL*.

"Josie," Melody cried, "Carson Daly tried to kill us tonight, and I think it has something to do with our music!"

Josie considered her words a moment, then said, "Why do you call it 'our music'?"

Frustrated, Valerie strode over to the mirror. "Because it's . . . are you even listening?"

"You bet I am," Josie said. "I've been listening very carefully. And you know what I hear? I hear someone glomming on to my talent. And my credit. 'Our music.' Hah! I basically write all of it."

Val looked stunned, but she was insulted, too. "No," she said firmly, narrowing her eyes at Josie. "We write it together."

"Oh. Okay." Josie patted her hair in the mirror. "So if we're doing equal amounts of work, why isn't the band called *Valerie* and the Pussycats?"

Valerie looked devastated. "I knew it!" she shouted. "You've been thinking this all along."

Josie ignored her and dug around in her makeup bag.

"I'm just . . . backup to you!" Valerie went on.

"But you're good, solid backup," Josie said sincerely. Then she threw back her head and roared.

Valerie recoiled from the person who looked like her best friend. Maybe aliens had come and taken over her body while they were away. Maybe she was suffering from a strange big city viral infection that made people just plain mean against their will.

But this couldn't be Josie, their Josie, the

one who'd said "Let's promise that we'll always be friends. Friends first, and a band second." That Josie would never act this way. It went beyond even the worst Val's paranoid imagination had conjured up in the past few days.

"But you know," Josie went on, lining her eyes in black pencil, "if this whole band thing doesn't work out, I can probably get you work as my bodyguard."

Josie laid down the eye pencil and threw some fake punches. Laughing at the look on Val's face.

Valerie didn't easily cry. But this . . . She couldn't control the tears welling up in her eyes. She turned and fled the room.

"Hey!" Josie called after her, "Remember what your stupid anger book says: 'Good people don't get angry.' "

Melody looked as if she was about to cry, too. She reached for Josie, pleading with her: "Josie, don't do this. We need to stick together now. . . ."

Josie held back a laugh. "Oh, my god. Melody's gonna cry. What's the matter, snugglebunny? Finally realizing the world's not all sunshine and rainbows?"

"Stop it. . . ."

Josie looked at her in pity. "Not everyone

gets a happy ending, muffin. And guess what? Puppies turn into dogs who get old and then they die."

Melody was shocked—she couldn't take anymore. Covering her ears, she burst into tears and ran out of the room.

"One day you'll thank me!" Josie shouted down the hall after her. "Of course, by then I won't be taking your calls!"

Smiling, Josie slammed the door and picked up her Discman again. Slipping on the headphones, she restarted the CD. She didn't know what it was about this music, but there was something really different about it. She loved the way it made her feel.

Josie's change in behavior had a major effect on everyone she knew.

Crying uncontrollably, Val dug through the stuff in her room until she found *12 Steps to Anger Management*. But this time she didn't read it—she tore the book into shreds.

Melody had fled to the streets, walking aimlessly until she found herself staring into a pet store window, crying as she looked at some puppies who would one day grow up.

Alan M. sat in the park, sadly strumming his guitar. Then he looked up and spotted Josie's face, smiling from another billboard—this one advertising "Concert Tomorrow!" He hung his head, too broken up to play.

Alexandra . . . well, she was actually happy that everyone was upset about Josie, and she snuggled into Alan M.'s shoulder, beaming happily. Okay, Alan M. didn't even notice right now, but he would soon, now that Josie was showing her true colors.

And poor Alexander stood all alone, crying in a doorway of a city shop. Actually, the store was Barney's, Alexander's new favorite up-scale clothing store, and he was bawling because they'd just locked the door and put a CLOSED sign in the window. It didn't have anything to do with Josie.

But he'd probably be really upset about her if he thought about it.

Meanwhile, Josie had gone for a long walk all by herself. All those annoying Riverdale people were getting her down. They were yesterday; Josie was now. She wished they'd just all go home and leave her alone.

As she walked along, she kept listening to herself singing that wonderful ballad on the CD Wyatt gave her.

But instead of calming her down, the way music usually did, she was starting to feel angry. She had her Discman cranked up loud.

*Val and Melody are not your friends!* A voice inside her head seemed to say. *Josie is the star! They're just riding your coattails! Val and Melody are out to get you! You should have a solo career!*

"That's the truth," Josie muttered as she walked on down the street. When she reached the other side, she passed a wall plastered with Josie and the Pussycats' album posters. She paused to look at the happy image of her and her friends—ha! Her ex-friends!

But then her scowl turned into a look of confusion. They did look so happy in those pictures. Was it an illusion? How could things like that be faked?

*You do all the work, they steal all the credit!* the voice in her head went on. *Val and Melody are not your friends. . . .*

Josie glared at the posters once again, then turned and walked on.

*They're trying to destroy you, Josie! You'll be better off without them! Valerie and Melody are mean, evil girls. . . .*

She was crossing the street now in the middle of a huge intersection. But she stopped short at the sight of an enormous Jumbotron video screen. MTV was on, playing the Pussycats' video. Josie looked up at their image in happier times. Okay, it was just a week ago, but they were happy.

*Val and Melody are not your friends!*

She turned away from the video, walking faster now. Something strange was going on in her mind—the music in her heart warring with these little voices in her head.

And all she wanted to do was get away.

Josie began to run, but she couldn't flee the thoughts and images in her brain.

*They're trying to destroy you, Josie!*

She ran past a guy selling knockoff Josie and the Pussycats ears on the street . . .

*Valerie and Melody are mean, evil girls.*

Past a Foot Locker, where a life-size Josie cutout tried to entice her into buying the new Leopard Puma athletic shoe . . .

As she ran down the street, a stray cat darted out in front of her. With a cry, she tripped and landed sprawled on the pavement.

The Discman warbled in and out, the CD messed up by the fall.

Josie lay there a minute, breathing heavily, trying to get her bearings. The little messenger bag she'd been carrying was torn, and the contents were spilled out across the sidewalk. She got to her knees and started to gather up her things: hairbrush, makeup case, sunglasses . . .

Suddenly her eye caught on something.

Her Riverdale bus pass. With the photo of

her with Valerie and Melody. The one they swore on on the plane. "Friends first . . ."

Josie ripped the headphones off her head and stared down at the CD player. What the hell was going on here?

Josie was determined to find out.

# 18

Josie burst into Valerie's hotel room. "Val! *Val!*"

But Valerie wasn't there. And the place was a mess.

Looking around, she found Alexandra on the bed, watching TV and gorging on room service. Her brother Alexander was sprawled on the floor, surrounded by wrappers and a bunch of junk food from the mini bar. He seemed awfully depressed.

He looked up when Josie entered the room. "Oh! The return of the sloopershtar . . ."

Josie groaned. He was obviously drunk! "What's going on? Where's Val?"

Alexander wagged an admonishing finger at her: "I heard somebody was being a 'See You Next Tuesday.' "

"What? Alexander—where are Val and Mel?"

"Since when do you care?" he snapped. He

swayed a little as he tried to sit up straight. "They're gone. An' I hope you're happy! No more band! Jus' like . . . the Beatles!" He started to cry. "Jus' like the Jackson 5 . . . Jus' like A Flock of Seagulls. . . ." Then he flapped his arms like wings and laughed. "Caw! Caw!"

Josie paced the room, trying to figure out what to do. She stared at the CD in her hand, thinking. "Okay. Here's what we have to do. We've gotta get out of this hotel and take this over to the recording studio. Right now!"

Alexander shielded his eyes. "Oh, so you're a god now? With your flashing idols? You're not a god! I am! I am god." He sighed in resignation. "There is no god." But then his blurry eyes caught sight of one of the mini bar treats—little tiny individually wrapped wedges of cheese. He snatched one up and held it high. "No god, but the Wee Brie!" he proclaimed.

Josie turned to Alexandra: "Okay, I never thought I'd be saying this to you, but—help."

Alexander smiled—and burped. "All hail the Wee Brie!"

Josie finally convinced Alexandra to help her pour her brother into a cab so they could all go to the recording studio. Thankfully, the place was empty.

Josie ran up to the mixing board. "Wyatt gave me this CD of our song," Josie explained. "And it was like, as soon as I heard it, I don't know . . ."

Alexandra swirled her Diet Coke can. "What, it sucked?"

Josie began flipping buttons, trying to figure out what she was doing. Then she slid all of the faders down to an even low level. "There's something on here. I'm positive." She pressed Play, and waited. Soon the first strains of Josie singing the ballad filled the room.

Alexandra made a face. "Sounds like a squirrel in a blender."

But for once Josie totally ignored Alexandra's digs. Josie slid up one of the faders. The music blared and distorted.

Alexandra covered her ears. Alexander fell off his chair.

Josie quickly moved the fader back.

Alexandra stood up to go.

"Wait—it's . . ." She chose another fader. "This one."

As she did, the music dropped out completely.

"Thank god," Alexandra said.

Then they heard . . .

*"Val and Melody are not your friends!"*

Josie's jaw dropped.

*"Josie is the star! You do all the work, they steal all the credit!"*

"Oh, my god, that's Mr. Moviefone!" Alexandra exclaimed. "How did you get him to put that on there?" She narrowed her eyes at Josie. "You slept with him!"

"What are you talking about?!" Josie exclaimed. "This is on our CD! Underneath the music!"

"Subliminal messages!" Alexander exclaimed. "The Wee Brie hears all. Behold the power of cheese!"

"Wyatt put them there," Josie said, realizing it as she said the words out loud. "To brainwash me."

"Shah, don't listen," Alexander whispered to his Wee Brie.

Alexandra popped open another Diet Coke and feigned a dramatic horror movie cue. "Duh-dum-dum!" Then she laughed. " 'Brainwashing.' . . . Okay." She pretended to be terrified. "Ooh . . . Help us, we're all being brainwashed!"

Alexandra sipped her Diet Coke and smiled.

"Diet Coke is the new Pepsi One."

Josie studied the fader that was up on the board. The paper tape above it was marked "MS."

Josie tried to figure out what it stood for. "MS . . . Main . . . system? Music . . . sequence?"

Thinking hard, she gazed out into the studio. She couldn't help but see the MegaSound, illuminated by a lone spot of light.

*Yes!* She scrambled out of the booth and hovered over the MegaSound. Alexandra poked at her brother with a drumstick. He drunkenly swatted it away, laughing. Josie shushed them! Then she turned on the MegaSound, and it hummed to life.

Then she pressed Play.

Nothing happened.

"Maybe you broke it," Alexandra suggested.

"Oooh!" Alexander crooned. "You're going to get in trouble."

Josie ignored them and fiddled with some knobs. Finally they could hear, loud and clear, Mr. Moviefone's voice coming through the MegaSound machine:

*"Josie and the Pussycats are the best band ever! They are totally jerkin'! You must buy their CD! You have to see them in concert. . . ."*

Josie's eyes widened.

*"You also have to buy Steve Madden shoes."*

173

*Wait a minute!* Josie just looked confused. *What did shoes have to do with our music?*

*"Heath Ledger is the new Matt Damon! You're nobody without an Abercrombie & Fitch vintage tee!"*

Josie gasped in amazement as she realized what was going on. "They're selling things through our music!"

*"Josie and the Pussycats are the best band ever!"*

"They're selling *us* through our music?"

Alexandra's eyes gleamed. "I *knew* there was a reason you were so popular!"

"I want a vintage tee!" Alexander shouted. "An' Heath Ledger!"

Josie stopped the MegaSound. She'd turned deathly pale. "Oh, my god. It's my fault. Everything. People dressing the same . . . buying the same stuff. I sold it to them. I'm a . . . trend pimp!"

But now her shock was turning to anger. She turned to Alexander and Alexandra. "Well, it stops here. I am nobody's pimp. And I'm not letting Fiona and Wyatt get away with this. We're going to the police. And we're taking this with us!"

She got behind the MegaSound machine and started to push. She couldn't even budge it. She glanced around. Maybe it was because no one was helping.

"Are you guys gonna help me or—"

And that's when she saw that they had company. Fiona and a group of her thugs.

"Oh, I'll help!" Fiona said with a laugh.

Josie gulped. This was not good.

# 19

"All right, the event I know everyone's been waiting for is finally here...." Carson Daly was doing his thing on a special live *Total Request Live*, only he looked a little beat up tonight. His arm was in a sling. He told everybody at the studio he'd hurt it playing rugby. "One night only ... The worldwide live debut concert of Josie and the Pussycats!"

Kids in the MTV studio audience cheered. The band's second single played as images of the girls from their video flashed on the studio flatscreens.

"Live at the Mega-Arena, with a simultaneous global Web cast!" Carson announced. "Log on to our Web site for details. And remember—you won't hear a note without your Josie 3-D-X headphones, so pick some up! I know I bought two!"

He held up the Josie cat-ear headphones. And put two pairs on his head. The studio audience put theirs on, too.

At the Mega-Arena, the parking lot was packed with fans having pre-concert tailgate parties. It was like a Grateful Dead show, only instead of everyone wearing tie-dye, they were all dressed in leopard. And everyone was wearing Josie headphones.

In an underground control room beneath the stage, Alexander and Alexandra sat nervously on a couch, closely monitored by a guard. They watched as another guard led Josie out of her star dressing room. She was in an elaborate, glitzy stage costume—and she looked miserable.

Fiona was just waiting for her. "Aw, look at the pouty girl. Boo-hoo. Well, you'd better snap out of it, Red, because you've got a show to put on.

Josie looked at her as if the woman had totally lost her mind—which she quite possibly had. "Are you kidding? There's no way I'm gonna play. Help you send messages to those kids? Forget it. I'm done."

"Oh, look who's all principled all of a sudden," Wyatt said. "You didn't seem to mind when your song hit number one."

Fiona stepped closer to Josie. "You should kiss my cellulite-free derriere for all I've done for you. I made you a rock star. Tell me you don't love that." She pointed up at the stage.

Josie listened. They could hear the crowd chanting above. Shouting for the Pussycats. Calling Josie's name.

It was tempting.

She turned back to Fiona. "I said forget it. Find yourself another girl."

Fiona sighed, annoyed. "Yeah, see I would—but everybody's already here. Too bad. But maybe all you need is a little more incentive."

Wyatt waved at a burly thug, who pulled aside one of the backstage curtains to reveal . . .

Val and Melody. Their hands were tied. The thug shoved them into the middle of the room.

"I found two little girlies who thought they could skip out on their hotel bill," Wyatt said.

"Val! Mel!" Josie cried, trying to get to them.

Melody struggled to hold out her hand. "Josie—"

But Valerie shushed her. "Don't talk to her!" Then to Fiona, she said, "Yeah, right. You think Miss Diva's gonna care if you do something to us?"

Oh, no! Josie realized. They still believed brainwashed Josie was the real Josie. "Listen to me!" she shouted. "I didn't mean any of that stuff I said! Wyatt and Fiona were putting sub-liminal messages in our—"

"Can it, Rusty! Your story's boring!" Fiona interrupted. "Wyatt, show the two young ladies what we have for them this evening."

"Gladly, my dear." He strode over to the stage curtain to reveal . . . A new car! Shiny, red, and revolving on a game-show platform.

"A car?" Melody exclaimed. "Val, I won a car!"

"No, you didn't win a car!" Fiona snapped.

"Oh, my god, Val—*you* won a car!"

Fiona looked as if she was going to burst into flames. *"No one won a car!!"* Then she collected herself and explained her little plan. "The car is about to be part of history." To Josie she added, "Mel and Val's history—*if* you decide not to play tonight."

Josie was totally confused.

To illustrate her point, Fiona aimed a remote at a nearby monitor. A clip from MTV News came on.

"This is Serena Altschul with breaking news. The Josie and the Pussycats debut concert was unexpectedly canceled when an automobile exploded in the stadium parking lot. The pas-sengers were identified as Valerie Brown and Melody Valentine, two of the founding mem-bers of the popular rock band. Examiners on the scene were quoted as saying 'the two died a slow, fiery death inside that four-wheeled hellpit.' "

The screen showed footage of a horrible car wreck.

Josie gasped.

"We are told Josie will be releasing a statement to the press within the hour to comment on this tragedy."

Wyatt turned to Josie, pretending to take notes: "Yes, Josie? What are your comments? We're *so* curious. . . ."

But Josie was speechless, horrified, as she watched Fiona's thugs force Valerie and Melody into the car. Once inside, the girls gazed out the car window, completely helpless.

"Hmm," Wyatt said, as if trying to decide between the blue tie or the gray. "Play the show, roast your friends? What's a girl to do?"

Josie glared at Wyatt. She couldn't believe what a total fake he was, how she'd been so duped by his concern for the band's success. She wanted to tell him and Fiona to stuff their concert.

But she couldn't. She didn't have a choice.

Josie walked over to her guitar and put it on, then turned back to Fiona, holding up her hands in angry defeat.

Fiona smiled gleefully.

"See, Val?" Melody said. "She still likes us."

"Oh, Mel," Josie said. "Of course I do! You guys are my best friends on the planet. And I know you don't treat friends the way I treated you. But, believe me, if I could go back in time, I'd take it all back."

Melody nodded, bummed. "That would be cool." Then she smiled. "If I could go back in time, I'd wanna meet Snoopy."

Smiling, Josie walked over toward the car where the girls were being held prisoner. "Mel. I love that about you. How you think everything is possible and the world is such a great place. Because, you know what? It is. And I'm sorry if for one second I made you think it wasn't."

"And Val . . ."

Val wouldn't even look at her.

"Val, you bought me my first guitar. And yeah, we may have started this band together, but the only reason we made it this far is because of you. I don't care if we're 'Josie and the Pussycats' or 'Valerie and the Pussycats' as long as we're together. You're my sister, Val. I love you."

For a moment, Valerie still wouldn't look at her, but then she did turn and face her—and her eyes were full of tears. "I love you, too, Jose. . . ."

"And I love you, Josie!" Melody said.

"And I love you, Mel!" Josie said.

"And I love you, Val!" said Melody.

"And I love—"

"I scream, you scream, we all scream for ice cream!" Fiona interrupted in disgust. "Everyone loves everyone—okay? Now let's get this show started."

Fiona drew aside another huge curtain, revealing a large hydraulic platform. The girls' band equipment and instruments were set up on it, backed by a wall of lights that spelled out JOSIE AND THE PUSSYCATS. Very Vegas-looking.

With a sigh of resignation—but happy to have her friends back—Josie climbed aboard.

# 20

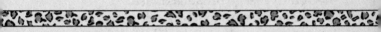

Josie could hear the sound of feet pounding on the stadium floor. The crowd was on its feet, chanting for Josie. Holding up lighters and "WE LOVE YOU JOSIE" signs. And everyone was wearing the leopard ears. They were ready to start the show.

Backstage Josie took her place and picked up her guitar. She watched as Fiona toyed with a pair of the leopard ears. She was a sick woman. What made her tick? Was it simply a power trip? Or did something else drive her extravagant evil?

"So, what is it this time, Fiona?" Josie asked her. "Cross-trainers? Pizza bagels? Lip gloss?"

A smug Fiona smiled and shook her head. "Oh, it's bigger. Much bigger this time."

Fiona laughed as joyfully as a kid with a new set of Barbie dolls as she flipped the hydraulic switch to ON. Slowly the whole platform began to rise.

Then she walked over to the MegaSound 8000 and held her finger over the PLAY button. Josie noticed that the MegaSound was connected to a large broadcast dish.

"It's gonna be hard to sell secret messages once your secret's out. . . ." Josie threatened.

"Oh?" Fiona asked. "And tell me, Cookie. Who will believe you? Who will get behind the ridiculous ramblings of one silly powerless girl?"

"We will!" a male voice cried out.

Fiona whirled around and watched in shock as a strange man ran in from the shadows. Well, limped in.

"Who the hell are you?" Fiona demanded.

"Someone you thought you'd gotten rid of." The dirty guy ripped off his scraggly beard—it was fake!

Josie gasped as she recognized one of the world's most famous faces—a face she thought no one would ever see in real life again.

Blond, boyish Les of Du Jour.

He was followed by three guys in full body casts. You couldn't see their faces, but from their accessories—and a monkey in a body cast—you could tell it was the rest of Du Jour.

"Oh, my god!" Alexandra cried.

Wyatt's face turned as white as a new Brooks Brothers dress shirt. "Les?"

"I tried to warn you guys." To Melody, he said, "The message on your mirror?"

"That was you?" Thrilled, she gushed to Val and Josie, "Du Jour was in my bathroom!"

"But I thought you guys were killed in a plane crash," Valerie said.

"That's what *I* thought. . . ." Fiona said angrily, her fists jammed on her hips. "Wyatt?"

Wyatt looked totally bewildered. The body-casted band shuffled about, obviously in a very bad mood. "We managed to land the plane just fine," Les said. "Unfortunately it was in the parking lot of a Metallica show."

Les gestured over at the guys. "The fans beat the crap out of us."

"Well, you don't look so bad," Melody said politely.

Les shrugged. "I knew the words to 'Enter Sandman.'"

There was a muffled sound from deep inside one of the body casts.

Les nodded. "That's right! She's *not* gonna get away with this! C'mon, guys! Let's get 'em!"

The casts shuffled ever so slowly toward Wyatt and Fiona. One guy completely tipped over.

"Goodness," Wyatt said dryly. "Won't someone please save us."

"Anyway . . ." Fiona turned back to the platform to get this concert underway. But now Josie was gone.

"Oh, now, come on!" Fiona whined.

Over at the car Mel and Val were watching poor Les. Suddenly the car door opened to reveal Josie, crouched down, trying to hide from Fiona. She motioned for them to be quiet as she reached in and untied them. But unfortunately . . .

"Boy, you almost got me." Fiona was standing right below the revolving car platform, smiling at Josie. "Curtain call, little one."

The girls turned and ran in the other direction. But the platform rotated them right back to Fiona.

"Honestly," Fiona scolded them. "Girls all over the world would kill to be in your handmade boots. And here you are, running away from it. Why? So you can crawl back to Riverdale and spend the rest of your lives being washed up with your friends Dopey and Meany?"

"What would you know about friends?" Josie asked her.

"Ouch!"

Fiona did a mocking imitation of a Pussycat handshake. Then laughed like it was the stupidest thing in the world.

Josie looked down at Fiona, who was cackling hysterically. Then Josie looked at Val and Mel, who nodded "go for it."

Josie dived off the platform at Fiona. The two women rolled around on the floor. Fiona's thugs ran over to help, but Fiona barked: "Back off! I can take this one myself!"

Josie used that moment of distraction to shove a handful of Chee-tos into Fiona's open mouth.

Fiona choked and spit them out. "Bitch!" She grabbed a large bowl and hit Josie in the head with it. As Josie went down, Fiona leapt at her.

Fiona and Josie were on their feet now, circling each other like wrestlers, feinting and ducking, waiting to see who would throw the first punch.

Fiona took the challenge and slapped Josie across the face. Josie slapped Fiona back. Then they just started slapping each other wildly. Scratching at each other. Pulling hair. A world-class catfight.

Valerie ran over to help Josie.

Wyatt stepped in front of her. "I don't think so."

Val smiled. "Wyatt . . . you messed with the wrong girl."

Fear flashed across Wyatt's face before Val

pulled his jacket up and over his head and started pummeling him.

Meanwhile, Melody was crazed, kickboxing Fiona's thugs. She'd come a long way from the innocent girl she was in Riverdale.

"Who wants a piece?!" she shouted.

*Slam!* She booted some dude in the jaw with a wicked roundhouse kick.

"Who's next?!" Melody shouted. "C'mon, bring it!"

The sight of the pert young blonde gone wild scared the pants off the other thugs, and they all ran away.

Melody looked down at the one she just dropped. "Oh, my god . . . are you okay? I'll get you an ice pack."

Out in the stadium the kids were getting restless. Two boys looked totally bored and annoyed. One looked at his ticket stub, then at his watch. "You know, if they're gonna start at nine, they should put nine on the ticket, not eight. . . ."

"Every show, man," his friend agreed. "What the hell always takes so long?"

Val was swinging Wyatt around by the arm. She tossed him toward a roped-off area, so he bounced back toward her—and like a pro wrestler, she clotheslined him. *Wham!* He dropped from view.

"God, that felt good!" Valerie exclaimed.

Meanwhile, Josie and Fiona tumbled over the main console in the control room, and technicians jumped out of their way. They landed behind the control board, looking a little scratched up and disheveled. They were surrounded by video monitors of the crowd, all wearing the Josie ear headphones cheering for the show to start.

Fiona snatched up a nearby electric guitar and held it like a baseball bat. "You know, I never liked you," she told Josie.

"That's because you have a problem with women," Josie replied. "You're completely threatened by them. It's why you surround yourself with men. Think about it. *Do* you have any close female friends?"

"Shut up!" Fiona cried. She swung the guitar at Josie, hard. It missed, but Josie looked a little nervous.

"It's nothing to be ashamed of," Josie said. "You're just not a girls' girl."

Fiona stopped swinging and glared murderously at Josie.

"Oops, touched a nerve, huh?" Josie said.

"Now what? You going to kill me with the guitar? Oooh. Then who's gonna get up and sing? You need me, remember?"

Fiona came at Josie, raising the guitar overhead. She laughed, because now she had Josie backed into a dead end. "Need you?" Fiona cracked. "I never needed *you*. I just needed someone to wear the ears. Doll, I created you. And you'd better believe I can destroy you, too"

Josie was trapped. She had nowhere to run.

Fiona smiled. "And I don't have a problem with women. I just have a problem with you!"

Josie cowered as Fiona raised the guitar over her head to deliver the final blow. But as Fiona slammed it down, Josie dived out of the way—and the guitar crashed down on the Mega-Sound 8000.

"I'm sorry," Josie said. "Did you need that?"

Fiona looked horrified. The MegaSound was severely damaged now, sparking and smoking. Fiona looked to the video monitors to see the kids in the stadium all taking off their headsets.

The kids in the crowd winced as loud static and feedback poured from their headphones. Annoyed, they started chucking them into the air.

The large broadcast dish, bearing the MegaRecords logo, pointed to the sky.

Kids around the country all began taking off their headphones.

Josie smiled as Fiona desperately tried to fix the MegaSound.

"Wyatt!" she shouted. "Fix it!"

In pain, Wyatt limped over and lifted the top off the machine. He waved away the smoke and tried to repair the damage. But it was pretty extensive. He pointed at a techie. "You, what's your job? Fix this!"

The techie wandered over and pounded on the machine a few times. Nothing happened.

"It's too late," Fiona whined. "They're taking off the ears. . . ."

Just then the light on the MegaSound flickered weakly. The voice of the Moviefone guy crackled over the MegaSound's speakers.

*"Fiona is the coolest girl in the world! Everybody loves Fiona! She's got the best hair, and the most awesome clothes! And she's so thin! I know I want to be just like Fiona. . . ."*

Everybody stared at Fiona, including Wyatt. Fiona tried to laugh it off.

"That's the secret message you wanted to send out?" Josie asked in disbelief. "That you're cool?"

"What? That'th not me—I thwear! I have no idea how that got on there!"

The next sound from the MegaSound was Fiona's voice. *"You're not doing it right!"*

There were sounds of a struggle:

"Hey!" Mr. Moviephone exclaimed. "Ow! That hurts!"

*"If I wath a guy I'd tho wanna ask her out. And if I wath a girl I'd wanna be her betht friend forever!"*

"What's wrong with your voice?" Alexandra asked.

*"We'd have thlumber parties and thtay up all night braiding each otherth' hair and having tickle fightth!"*

Josie and Val looked at each other. Then they burst out laughing. Everyone did.

Fiona couldn't take it anymore. "Oh, thure!" Fiona cried. "Laugh at me! Go ahead. You don't know what itth like! To be teathed and ridiculed every day of your life! 'Theven thilver thwans thwam thilently theaworth!' 'Thee thells thee thells by the theethore!' I tried, didn't I?! All I ever wanted watht to be popular. Whatht tho bad about that?"

Before anyone could respond, Wyatt spoke up. "Oh, my god. . . . Lisa?"

Fiona whirled around. "What did you call me?"

"Lisa Brecker? 'Lithping Litha'?"

"That was . . . my nickname from thchool," Fiona admitted.

". . . Huntingdon High School?"

"Yeth . . ."

"Lisa, it's me!" Wyatt exclaimed. "Wally! White-Ass Wally!"

"White-Ath Wally? The Albino kid? Thatth impothible! I mean, firtht of all, he wasthn't Britith."

Wyatt suddenly dropped his accent: "I'm not. I just started talking this way because I thought it would make me more attractive."

"And he wath tho pale. . . ."

"Makeup!" Wyatt explained. "Ever since we graduated, all I've been doing is changing myself to be more likeable! Cosmetics, diets, surgeries. . . ."

"I learned to thpeek without a lithp!" Fiona said proudly.

"Look!" He reached up to his beautiful thick hair—and ripped it off. It was a wig—he was really completely bald.

"Look!" Fiona cried, reaching into her mouth. "A falthe tooth!" Fiona smiled at him. "I can't believe it'th you! Ithn't thith the thrrangetht cointhidenth?"

Beaming at each other, both on the verge of

sobbing, they joyfully ran toward each other's arms.

But then Wyatt stopped just in front of her. "Wait . . ." He exhaled, letting out his large gut. In fact, it was so large, it hung out over his belt. "Whew! I've been holding that in for the past fifteen years!"

Fiona slipped her arms around his ample middle. "I think . . . it'th thexthy."

"Ohhh. This is so romantic," Melody said.

"Uh, I guess. . . ." Valerie said.

"Yeah, in a creepy ironic sort of way," Josie added.

Wyatt and Fiona tentatively, awkwardly held hands.

"She's right," Alexander said. "All this time I've been spending money on expensive clothes, trying to impress people—but it never made me happy. Happy is on the inside! I am not what I wear!"

Alexander began stripping off his clothes. Alexandra rolled her eyes.

"Accept yourself, sister!" Alexander said. "You don't need to throw yourself at men for validation! You should start by getting happy with who you are!"

"Oh, please," Alexandra said. "Unlike you bunch of whack jobs, I'm perfect just as I am!"

"Holy cow!" someone suddenly exclaimed.

"That girl's got a skunk on her head!"

Agent Kelly strode into the room, pointing at Alexandra, in shock. Then he took a closer look.

"Oh, jeez. It's just your hair, sorry. But that's messed up."

Alexandra put her hand over her hair, suddenly embarrassed. "I'm . . . perfect just as I am."

Agent Kelly looked around. "What's going on in here? Aren't you girls supposed to be playing a concert? The crowd is going nuts!"

They could hear the crowd chanting for Josie.

"Who are you?" Josie asked.

"Agent Kelly. I'm with the government."

"Oh, thank god!" Josie cried. "Did you know that Fiona and Wyatt were using that machine to send subliminal messages through our music? They were trying to create an army of mindless teenagers! To make them buy things and even control their thoughts?"

Agent Kelly pretended to be shocked: "They what?!"

"Oh, come on!" Fiona exclaimed. "You knew about thith from the very be—"

"Gentlemen, arrest that woman and that man!" Agent Kelly ordered his men.

"What?!" Fiona screamed.

"On charges of conspiracy against the youth of America!" Agent Kelly declared.

"You can't be theriouth!"

"I am serious, ma'am. This is a very serious offense."

The agent clapped cuffs on Fiona and Wyatt. Agent Kelly leaned in to Fiona and whispered "Sorry, Fiona. They busted us. We needed somebody to take the fall."

"You bathtard!" she cried.

"Besides," Agent Kelly said, "After the concert we were shutting down your entire operation anyway. We found out subliminal advertising works much better in movies."

Wyatt leaned toward Fiona, shy: "Maybe after we get out of prison, we could go for pizza?"

Fiona smiled her gap-toothed smile, and they held each other's handcuffed hands as Agent Kelly led them away. The other agents left to round up the rest of the bad guys, leaving Josie and her friends alone under the stadium.

Alexander stepped up, completely naked now, holding a blue bass in front of himself.

"Well, now that you guys are done saving the world . . . I think there's the small matter of a half a million kids out there . . . who need to feel happy on the inside."

He lifted the bass up to hand it to Val. She

grimaced and waved it back down to where it covered him up.

From above, they heard chanting.

"Come on," said Val. "Let's do it."

Melody twirled her sticks. She was ready. Val strapped on her old bass and stepped toward the hydraulic stage.

But then Josie stopped them. "We can't."

# 21

"What?" Valerie shrieked.

"We can't go on," Josie said. "Can't you see, guys? The only reason they're out there is because of Fiona's messages. It's . . . what I thought. We didn't earn this. They never really liked us or our music."

The three Pussycats thought about this for a moment.

"So what are we gonna do?" Val said. "Just pack up and go home?"

Josie didn't say anything.

"Okay," said Val. "If we go out there, what's the worst that could happen? They boo us off the stage?"

Melody smiled, super positive. "We've been booed off lots of stages!"

"She's right," Val agreed. "So what? We'll go back to playing in bowling alleys like the old days. The three of us. And that's all that matters."

"Remember?" Melody said. " 'Friends first. . . . ' "

Josie smiled at them. "And a band second."

They did a Pussycat handshake.

Together, they were ready to rock.

Out in the stadium the lights dimmed. The crowd roared in anticipation. Spotlights swirled over the audience. As the music swelled, the huge cat ears on top of the stage lit up. The place went nuts.

Josie and the Pussycats rose up from beneath the stage. Kids surged forward, crazy, as the lights came up to reveal the girls. The crowd was still roaring.

Josie was overwhelmed. She tentatively stepped up to the mike. As she did, the entire crowd put their cat ear headphones back on, eager for the show to start.

Josie stared out at them—all those ears. All those faces looking up at her. It was too weird.

"You know what? I'm gonna take these off."

She took off her cat ears. The crowd took their ears off, too.

Josie put hers back on.

The crowd copied her.

"Whoa," Josie whispered.

"Okay . . . look," she said into the mike. "I know you're all here because you heard something you liked on our CD. So we thought maybe we'd start off with something you haven't heard."

Val smiled at Josie. Mel nodded.

"It's cool if you like it, or even if you don't," Josie said. "Just decide for yourselves. We're playing it because it means something to us. Maybe it'll mean something to you, too."

She looked down at her guitar for a moment. "This is for someone who said he believed in me." Nervously she added, "Kind of wish he was here now."

Slowly she began to strum her guitar. Singing a few bars quietly at first . . . and then she nodded to Mel, who counted off "One! Two! Three!"

Josie and the Pussycats ripped into the full song—upbeat and raw and not dressed up or faked out by any strange machinery. It was the real thing.

The crowd did not go wild.

Josie and Val traded glances. Were they awful? Okay? They couldn't really tell, so they just quit worrying about it. This was their one night to shine in front of a giant crowd, so they just sang and played and had the time of their lives.

But then something miraculous happened. The crowd started to get into it. Bobbing their heads to the music. Some were even dancing. By the second chorus, the energy was spreading through the crowd. Except for the hysterical hometown girls, who sneered and pushed their way out of the crowd, leaving. Guys were taking their shirts off and throwing them onstage.

They got to the breakdown section, then far off at the back of the floor, someone began jumping up and down.

"Josie!!!"

Heads turned to check it out. It was Alan M. He'd heard what she just said, and he was pretty sure Josie was talking about him. At least he hoped she was.

But he was as far away from the stage as humanly possible—a speck in the crowd. There was no way Josie could see or hear him.

But Alan M. desperately needed to see her. And then suddenly he figured out a way: crowd surfing.

Within seconds, he was passing over the heads of the crowd, being carried along on a sea of people. "Josie!" he cried. "*Josssiieee!!!*"

During a break in the music, Josie heard her name. But not just shouted out the way her regular fans said it. There was something special about it, and familiar.

Scanning the crowd, she spotted Alan M. surfing his way toward her on the crowd.

"Alan M.?" Josie said in disbelief.

"Josie!" he shouted, waving frantically at her.

"What are you doing here?!"

Alan M. struggled to stay up. "I just wanted to tell you—even though you don't feel the same way about me as I do about you, and even though you didn't come to my gig—"

"Your gig?" Josie exclaimed. "Wyatt told me it was canceled!"

"That jerk!"

"But wait—what do you mean?" Josie asked. " 'I don't feel the same way about you as you do about me'?"

He was almost at the stage now.

*That's what I came here to tell you!* Alan M. shouted. *"JOSIE MCCOY, I—"*

*Thud!* The crowd dropped him.

Josie winced. But a couple of guys put him back up and surfing again.

*"I love you!"* he shouted.

Josie couldn't believe it. "You do?! Alan M. I love you, too! I always have!"

*"You* do? Why didn't you say something?"

"We're such good friends. I didn't want to screw things up."

"Josie!" Alan M. shouted. "You're beautiful

and talented and everything a guy could ever want. I totally wanna screw things up!!!"

Josie beamed; the crowd cheered.

And finally Alan M. was deposited at the foot of the stage. Quickly he scrambled to his feet and faced Josie. "I love you."

Josie smiled at him, tears welling up in his eyes. "I love you too."

And with that, they threw their arms around each other and kissed—just about the greatest kiss anyone in the stadium had ever seen. The crowd cheered and whistled.

Then Josie and Alan M. broke apart, laughing and a little embarrassed.

"You know, I think someone stole my wallet in there," Alan M. said.

"Sorry."

Just then Valerie stepped up to them, still playing. "Uh . . . Josie?"

"Hmm?"

Val gestured to the crowd.

"Oh—right!"

She turned to Mel, signaling her to cut off the breakdown—and then the song kicked in again. The crowd was really into it now.

The Pussycats loved it, smiling to each other as they played. Alan M. watched from the wings, proud, fantasizing about a few duets he'd like to try with Josie.

And Alexander and Alexandra lived out a fantasy by dancing backstage with the guys from Du Jour.

And as for Josie—all the insanity of the past few days evaporated as she got down to what it was really all about—the music, clean and pure, surging from somewhere deep down inside of her—music that no technology could ever duplicate or improve upon—and her heart soared as she sang like a bird does . . . not for ratings or record deals or TV appearances or applause, but because it's just gotta sing.

The kids in the audience listened, really listened, as Josie sang about friendship and love and all the things in life that really mattered . . . and they knew that for once, they were hearing something real.

And the place rocked.

# CABOT & CABOT INC

For Immediate Release.

## JOSIE and the PUSSYCATS!

Say step back to Backstreet Boys . . . just a sec to 'N Sync . . . uno momento Ricky Martin and "chill out" 98°!

Get ready for the most "purr-fectly" awesome band in the stratosphere—get ready to say "Meow!" to **JOSIE and the PUSSYCATS!**

From Riverdale—where the chicks definitely gotta rock—come three of the most talented, entertaining and just plain awesome girls you've ever met—Josie, Val, and Melody! They're Josie and the Pussycats—and they're ready to take over your world in a big time way.

These three mega-hot musicians have spent years "purr-fecting" their craft, writing songs (yes, they actually do the writing themselves!) and working to create the kind of music that moves them—pure rock 'n roll, edgy, strong, loud and melodic, with lyrics that really speak to the heart of a generation. Josie and the Pussycats are like nothing you've ever heard or seen before.

The spiritual leader of the band is Josie Mc-Coy, lead vocalist and guitarist. With her fiery red hair and serious "tough girl" attitude, Josie makes a major statement when she steps out onto the stage. But she's no poser—she's been taking guitar lessons since she was a little girl, and writing poetry and songs since she could talk. And although she may seem like the natural leader, Josie's always ready to tell you exactly how important her two best friends are to the group. "We're friends first, and a band second," says Josie. "These girls are my best friends. Val bought me my first guitar, and the only reason we made it was because of her and Melody. They're my sisters and I love them."

Although Josie always knew that music was her first love, she spent years working at uninspiring jobs so she'd have the money to invest in The Pussycats—she worked in a CD store (where she studied all types of music, and totally cemented her love affair with rock 'n roll) and as a waitress (where she dropped things, a lot). But now that she and her true blue best friends have reached the ultimate level of super stardom, Josie is ready to put those days behind her, and to concentrate totally on making music—the best music she can create! "Life is too short," she says. "We're musicians, and we should be playing music. Even when things were tough for us, I always used to say, 'If life gives you lemons, you make lemonade!" And that positive attitude flows over everything she does—it even reaches out to her fans. "It's cool if they like the music or even if they don't," she says. "We're playing it because it means something to us and maybe it'll mean something to them too."

To Val and Melody, Josie is a true friend—a loyal, honest, and serious girl who would do anything for her bandmates.

While Josie rips through her guitar solos, tall and tough Valerie Brown—you can call her Val—keeps the group grooving with her smooth bass playing. An expert in Martial Arts (she's been taking lessons since she was a kid, and even spent some time as a Karate instructor for Riverdale's "youthfully challenged" population), Val originally thought she might pursue a career as a sensei. But Josie (and music) came calling, and Val's been hooked ever since. But even she can't believe how fast the Pussycats have flown up the charts. "Maybe it isn't strange at all," she says. "I mean, isn't this how it always happens? Some band you've never heard of comes from out of nowhere and suddenly gets huge for no apparent reason. Maybe it only seems strange because this time, the number one band is us!"

When Val isn't writing music or practicing her bass plucking, she's busy working out—Valerie is a serious athlete who's run in the Riverdale 10K and thinks nothing of an afternoon of rock climbing. There's no sport in the world that Valerie hasn't conquered. She's the Pussycat most likely to knock you out!

Keeping the band's back beat pounding is Melody Valentine—and although her drumming may be loud and powerful, her personality is all sweet and sincere. In fact, Melody never dreamed she'd be beating the skins in a rock band—she was certain she would become a veterinarian or an Animal Rights activist. For years, Melody had been a familiar sight on Riverdale streets—her "Honk If You Love Hugs!" signs were legend.

But underneath that sweet exterior beats the soul of a drummin' warrior, and once she hooked up with her friends Josie and Val, she'd found her calling—her buds call her the true soul of the Pussycats. And now that she's a member of one of the hottest bands in the country, how does this world-famous rock babe behave? "When fans scream at me, I scream back," she says.

With the success of their first single, "Pretend to Be Nice," the girls have seen their entire lives change—they're driven around in limos, they make guest appearances on MTV (they're totally tight with host Carson Daly) and they travel all over the world. But no matter where their fame takes them, they will always remain true to their music and to one another. They'll always remember that vow they made so many years ago—friends first, a band second.

Now for the big question—what's with the leopard prints and cat ears? Well . . . to be honest . . . the girls haven't really told us what's up with that. In fact, whenever we ask, they start yelling at us and calling us all sorts of names and it makes us crazy, because you know, we're only trying to help and everything! And you know, we're not bad people either . . . so what if we don't play instruments or wear stupid cat ears! We work hard, and we're dedicated . . . we just don't know what these girls want from us! Day after day, we come into the office and do everything we can to promote Josie and the Pussycats and what do they do—they make fun of us. And sometimes, the girls even have to hold Val back from whacking us! This makes us crazy! So if you really want to know, you're going to have to call and set up an interview because we've done all we can!

For More Information Call
   Alexander or Alexandra Cabot, 555-3434.

# So You Wanna be a Rock Star? Here's How!

Josie and the Pussycats are definitely an inspiring group—who wouldn't want to live the life of a rock 'n roll queen? Screaming fans, awesome parties, bodyguards, limos, private jets and all those hot celebrities you meet every day—this is a lifestyle you're going to want to emulate. So how can you form your very own super group or garage sensation? It's not as hard as you think—getting started is the easy part. (It's getting the record deal that's tough . . . but more on that later.)

But the first thing you have to do is decide exactly what kind of rock star you want to be. Do you want to be . . .

*A ROCK 'N ROLL REBEL?*

**A POP PRINCESS (OR PRINCE)?**

*A folksinger whose life and music make the world a better place?*

The fact of the matter is, it takes different skills and different styles to get down these three musical paths. Yeah, you've got to be able to sing, and it helps if you can write your own songs (although that's not as important for you pop babes—more on that later!) but that is where the similarities end.

So think long and hard . . . do you want to be rock stars, like Josie and the Pussycats? Do you want to fly to the heights of pop music fame, like Du Jour? Or do you want to play music in coffee shops, like Alan M.?

Have you decided? Good! Now let's make a plan!

## HOW TO BE A ROCK REBEL!

Take a good, hard look at Josie and the Pussycats. What do you see? Besides the cat ears.

Instruments!

Rock stars play instruments. Unless you want to be a lead singer—which is another story all together—you've got to play an instrument. Rock stars don't usually use recorded tracks, they don't lip synch, and they don't dance around like Britney or Christina . . . they rock and roll to real, live music.

So what are you going to play?

## GUITAR GODS & GODDESSES!

How do you get a guitarist to stop playing?
Put some sheet music in front of her!
That's just a little guitarist humor.

Learning how to play the guitar isn't rocket science—if you've got the music in your heart you can probably get it to move up into your fingers. Lots of people teach themselves how to play guitar in the privacy of their own bedrooms, and lots more take lessons. But first, you need a guitar.

To be a real, live rock star, you need a real serious guitar. A real serious *electric* guitar, if possible—hey, how cool will you look strumming a cool, sleek Fender or Richenbecher? Those really awesome black ones . . . or maybe a really hot red one that's cut out to look like a star . . . the choices are endless. But then again, a good acoustic guitar will work too, especially when you're just learning to play. No need to blast out a sour note to the whole household! Where to purchase your first guitar you ask (cuz you know once you start collecting them, you'll never stop!) You can get great deals on guitars on the Internet (eBay, anyone?) or your local paper's classified ads.

Now that you've got your guitar, you've got to learn to play the darn thing. You have three choices: take guitar lessons from a professional, buy a guitar songbook and figure out songs yourself, or wing it and improvise your own personal playing style. You can find a guitar teacher through word-of-mouth—this is your chance to network with that cool guitar player in your school or work—or by searching bulletin boards at supermarkets, record or instrument shops. And of course there's always the Yellow Pages. If you opt to learn "by the book," you can purchase the guitar songbook for your favorite band. Make sure to get the kind that shows you where to place your fingers on the fretboard, then strum away. For option #3, just pick up the guitar and start noodling. You might come up with something that sounds good if you just keep playing long enough.

Once you start taking guitar lessons, you've got to get a guitar player's attitude. That means you think, talk, and obsess over nothing but your guitar. You start drawing pictures of it on your notebook. You start using words like "fretboard" and "power chord" in your daily conversation. You start thinking about how amazing Jimi Hendrix was, and how Ike Hanson is a god. You stress over things the rest of the world never even thinks about—like, do you have a guitar string to replace the one you broke the other day, or do you need a new glitter guitar strap.

Then you have to start dressing like a guitar player. You have to grow long bangs, so they can hang over your eyes when you're playing. You need to cut holes in the knees of your jeans. You need to find a pair of platform boots you can walk in without tipping over.

And you have to learn to strut.

Watch some old Heart videos and check out Nancy Wilson—watch the way she bounds across the stage. Watch the ways she kicks up her legs and spins around. You've got to do that! You've got to be able to take control of that stage! You can do it! You rule!

## *JOSIE—THE ULTIMATE GUITAR QUEEN!

When you watch Josie strut her stuff on stage, you know you're looking at one serious rock musician—she's one with her guitar, and she can make it majorly move and groove. She's most comfortable when she's playing guitar—it's one of her best friends. And she's got all the qualities of a great guitarist—she loves music, the spotlight, and making people happy. Put a guitar in her hands, and she can make it weep—she's proud of her skills and she's worked hard to get where she is. You know she'll do anything to stay on top—anything but sell out her principles and her beliefs, that is.

## BASS PATROL!

Are you quiet? Are you introspective? Do you tend to fade into the woodwork at parties? Then face it—the bass is the instrument for you.

The bass is not an intimidating instrument—hey, it's only got four strings, right? It's amazing what you can do with an E string! But the important thing to remember about being a bass player is this—you have to be mysterious. Check out some of your favorite bands and watch the bass player plucking her strings—notice how she hangs back a little, keeping to herself and concentrating on her groove? A bass player is not someone who loves the spotlight—a bass player is the backbone and balance to a band. Think about it—how many bass players can you even name? See what we mean?

Of course you can have a career as a bass player if you're funky and cool—that kind of bass player slaps their bass around, basically banging it and bending it to her earthquaking will. These bass players are in the minority. If you're pursuing the bass life, it helps if you're not much of a character—if you are a "personality," you might want to think about playing the guitar.

Bass players are also in demand—apparently there are not enough of them to fill all the bands in the world. Therefore, becoming a bass player may be your most practical choice—there will be plenty of work for you. Especially if you have your own amp.

**\*VAL—BASS ROYALTY!**

Let's face it—Val can be a little, shall we say, anti-social. She has anger management issues, she's always looking to hit someone with something, and she's always getting left behind. Val is the perfect bass player! Aside from her talent, which is major, she's got the perfect personality to shine with her bass. When things get tough, and she's feeling stressed, she knows she can find peace of mind by playing her instrument.

## WE GOT THE BEAT!

Ahh, drummers. The pounding heartbeat of the band.

And without question, the weirdest member of any rock group.

Hey, it makes perfect sense, doesn't it? After all, most drummers got their start banging on pots and pans and other peoples' heads. These are not stable people. These are not the type of people you want doing your taxes or operating on your pet cocker spaniel. These are muy crazy types!

Obviously, to practice drumming, you need a drum set. But the great thing is, to a drummer, all the world is a drum set. You can walk around your neighborhood banging on mailboxes, fire hydrants, and your neighbor's front door. You can take your drumsticks and beat the sofa, the kitchen counter or the TV set (this will really annoy your dad, but hey, you're a rock star—it's your job to annoy people!). You can also minimize damage by using special drum brushes—they're quieter and better to the furniture.

One really cool thing about being a drummer is that a good drummer can infiltrate any band—as long as you've got the talent, you'll be welcomed with open arms. Of course, practicing your drums could be a problem—no one really enjoys hearing a drummer practice, and you may have to install sound-proofed walls in your garage. This will also annoy your dad, who may not be that skilled with tools.

Drummers also need to "drum up" a little attitude—if you're too nice, you'll never get a drum solo. Remember Ringo Starr, of Beatles fame? He had to wait for years to get a drum solo of his very own. Who needs that? You want your drum solo now! Start talking about your drum solo with your bandmates—let them know this is something that is not negotiable. Remember—when it comes to drum solos, you can never be too nice!

## *MELODY: DRUM-DUM?

An unkind person might surmise that Melody is a little . . . brain challenged. When the going gets tough, she makes lemonade. When things get crazy, she stares at her toes and notices that they resemble a family of astronauts.

But Melody is definitely not stupid—far from it! And when it comes to playing drums, she's a total pro. She's actually the drummer of your dreams—she really knows how to bang out the beat.

## KEYBOARDS? WHY NOT?

You may notice that The Pussycats don't have a keyboard. You may notice that Bon Jovi does. What does this bode for all you keyboard players out there? Let's face it—in many rock bands today you're not that necessary, you're expendable, and that can wreak havoc on the self-esteem. But hey, in today's digital age, we hear keyboard players are once again reaching for their pinnacle of popularity, the Moog '60s. So don't quit those piano lessons Mom and Dad made you take. They may come in handy yet.

## LEAD SINGERS ALWAYS GET THEIR WAY!

You've been singing in the choir since you were three. You've been singing in the shower since you were two. You've been singing since you uttered your first words. Hey, you're the lead singer, and you're all that and a bag of fries on the side.

Lead singers should love singing, and be good at it, too. Taking voice lessons is a great idea;

singing in the choir or chorus couldn't hurt; singing into your hairbrush is a rite of passage.

But more important, the lead singer needs to have a serious lead singer attitude. Nothing is too good for the lead singer. The lead singer rules! You've got to believe it in your heart. A lead singer is God's gift to the world.

If you're looking to be the lead singer, you've got to get the look and the attitude. You've got to love being in the spotlight. You can't be too introverted or too shy—the lead singer wants to be noticed all the time, on stage and off!

So, you've got the talent—now you need the look.

*The Blonde Bombshell*: Many rock 'n' roll singers are blonde. This has been true throughout history. Courtney Love is blonde. Kurt Cobain was blonde. The guys in Goo Goo Dolls are blonde. Those lead singers in big hair heavy metal bands were blonde. Everyone in Hanson is blonde. Blondes reportedly even have more fun. You may want to be a blonde. If you weren't born a blonde, you may want to buy a bottle and make yourself blonde. You may want to pay a hairdresser to make you blonde. Blonde is good.

*Raven Haired Soul Singer*: Of course, dark

hair is nice too, and many lead singers have long, flowing brown locks. You may, of course, add some blonde highlights to your dark-brown coif—because, as we mentioned, blonde is good. But all those guys in Creed and Third Eye Blind have done quite well with their brown hair.

*Ab-Fab Red*: Josie's gotten far with her cool red hair and you can too—red hair is sizzling on stage, and a definite attention grabber.

*Other:* Sometimes, lead singers march to the beat of a different drummer (other than the one in their band, for example) and that beat takes them to hair color choices not usually found in nature—the lead singer of Green Day once had green hair, and you can too, with a little ingenuity. No Doubt's Gwen Stefani is always doing something new and inventive with her hair and look at her—she's crazy successful, and she dates Gavin Rossdale from Bush! How cool is that! Yes, rainbow colored hair just might be the thing for you. Be warned however: if you are currently employed in a job where you meet the public, you might want to think twice before dying those locks green, blue, or magenta—managers tend not to understand such fashion bravery. But if you're self-employed, or you work in a record store—get a bottle of Manic Panic or Punky Colors and go for it!

## DRESS THE PART!

A lead singer also has to think about their "look" in terms of clothes. Take a look at your favorite lead singer. Look at how he or she is dressed. You can bet your life that your idol isn't wearing polo shirts and penny loafer. Oh no. Your favorite lead singer looks totally cool, from top to toe.

Lead singers want attention—that's why they became lead singers in the first place. So if you want to join their ranks, you've got to seek out the spotlight too.

Glitter and glam play important roles in the lead singers wardrobe. Whether you're sporting leopard print pants or glittery tops, you're out to make an impression. No muted earth tones for you! A lead singer knows he or she looks hot in gold, silver, and red.

Of course, certain lead singers wore flannel. They were in the minority.

And lots of lead singers wear black—black tee shirts and black jeans, with black platform boots. This look is especially cool if the songs you're singing are filled with angst. You'll simply look more angst-ridden if you're dressed in black.

But for the lead singer with attitude—find your own personal style then multiply it by 13!

## YOU WRITE THE SONGS!

One thing that separates rock musicians from their pop music counterparts is this: rock musicians write their own songs! This is a very important badge of honor for rock musicians. Rock musicians want you to know—the words they're singing are their own.

So, what are you gonna write about?

Anything and everything! Write a love song about your crush, write a sad song about the love who did you wrong, write an angry anthem about the state of the world and what can be done to fix it! A true songwriter can find inspiration everywhere he or she looks.

But wait . . . you're thinking, I can't write a song! There's no way I could ever write a song!

Of course you can. And you can practice by reading and writing everyone's least favorite

English assignment—poetry. Write poems about how you're feeling inside, then read them aloud—hey, that sounds suspiciously like a song, doesn't it?

Now that you've written a few lyrics, sit down with your guitar or your keyboard and start playing—any little melody will do. Sing your words as you play. Pretty good huh?

Songwriting takes lots of patience and practice. You can write songs alone, or with your bandmates—whichever feels more efficient. If you and your bandmates really get along, you'll have a blast writing songs together. If you don't . . . you're going to get a big headache, so you might as well write when you've got some private time.

## GETTING YOUR ROCK BAND TOGETHER!

Once you've become an expert with your instrument (or your voice) you've got to find other, like-minded musical types to form a rock band. There are several ways to do this.

*Ask Around*! Simply talk to your friends (or people you see at school and work who are always air-drumming with headphones on) and mention that you want to start up a band. You might find musical soul mates you never knew existed.

*Put Up Flyers*! Use your graphic artist skills and create a flyer or poster announcing your intentions. Hang the flyers in the supermarket, the record store, the music store, the band room—anywhere prospective musicians might be hanging out.

*Take Out an Ad*! This costs money, which you may not have a lot of, but if you can scrape together a few bucks, place an ad in a music magazine.

*Hit the Net!* The Internet is a great tool that can help you reach out and touch millions of people in a minute—scary, huh? Post notices and mention your band in chat rooms—you never know . . . your very own bandmates may be out there, waiting for you.

## HOW DO YOU GET TO MADISON SQUARE GARDEN?

Practice, practice, practice.

Once you've got your band together, you have to start rehearsing together. Make no mistake—practice is key. The more you play, the better you'll get. You may have to be a little bit of a tyrant about the rehearsal schedule—you won't want anyone to get away with coming to practice late, or even worse, chatting and gossiping when you should be turning your amps up to 11 and wailing. Put your foot down—it takes work to make it to the top, and you want to be confident that you all agree that chart-topping success is 90% perspiration.

Make sure your rehearsal time is free and clear—do not schedule them on your lunch hour, or between classes. You need time to really get into practice mode. You don't want your drummer to suddenly say, "Oops, gotta get back to work!" in the middle of a serious set. That will get on your nerves and eventually, your band could break up because of it.

## FINDING A PLACE TO PRACTICE!

The garage, the basement, the band room at school, or a fully-equipped space which rents by the hour or day—these are some of your rehearsal space choices. Chances are, finding the a practice space will give you a migraine—you need a place where you can really crank it up and rock out, and you need a place that meets your (probably) meager budget. If you (or another member of your band) has supportive and understanding parents or roommates, you're golden!

## WHERE ARE YOU PLAYING?

Once you've practiced enough in the privacy of your rehearsal space, the time will come when what you really want to do is play live, in public—like, in front of real people.

One of the best ways to introduce people to your music is plan a gig of your own—throw yourself a huge party in your backyard or local community center. Get another band or two to play with you if you can. They can bring their pals, too. Invite everyone you know and let the fun begin. Chances are, a lot of your friends will be impressed and say nice things about you.

Booking other types of gigs can be tough— and finding the right place to showcase your music can be even tougher. Every member of the band has to be willing to get into the promotion end of the business—ask around, visit coffee shops, clubs, or any other venue that has a stage and might let you play on it. Never give up—get out there and meet people, kiss up if you have to—just make the contacts. Eventually, you'll find a venue that'll let you play.

## GET 'EM IN!

So you've got a venue, now you've got to get into the publicity business—you've got to advertise, let the whole world know where and when you're playing, and get 'em there to cheer you on.

Again, the Internet is great for this kind of publicity. Post notices everywhere you can, and get the word out. Make more flyers (does it feel like you're getting way too familiar with paper products? Good sign!) and hang them on every flat surface. (Some towns don't like this kind of advertising—make sure it's not illegal in your town or just stick with posting them on public bulletin boards.) Do a mailing—fold up your flyer into thirds, write an address on it, stick on a stamp and mail it to everyone you know—including that cousin you're not all that fond of. If you're really ambitious, you might want to put together a fan 'zine to let people know what you're all about—you're not a lip synching, choreographed bunch of droids, you're a real live rock band with opinions of your own. And of course, spread the word via your mouth—talk up your band to everyone you meet, get them excited. You might even want to hire yourself a manager, like Alexander Cabot . . . well, OK, maybe not like Alexander Cabot! You want to be a rock star—you've got to work hard to make it happen. Now go get busy while we talk to those people who want to follow their pop music bliss . . . this will only take a minute or two.

## POP 'N FRESH!

If you're looking to follow the Du Jour path to fame and fortune, if you want to be an all-singing, all-dancing, all-costumed pop group . . . can't we talk you out of it? No? Even after hearing about the subliminal messages? No? Gatorade is the next Snapple. Any problem with that? OK then, it's your life.

Boy pop groups come in two varieties: four member and five member. This has to do with vocal harmonies—pop groups owe much of their historical relevance to the old Motown groups of the 60s, and these groups all followed the strict four and five-part harmony structures.

Do not believe what pop groups tell you—they've all been put together in one way or another. Usually, someone holds auditions (this is how the Spice Girls got together) and chooses the members, who are then forced to spend all their time together so they can get to know one another and become best friends. In other cases, part of the group is put together, and then a friendship or family connection brings in another member, thus making it seem like the group formed spontaneously. There's nothing inherently wrong with being put together, by the way—although lots of boy bands seem to think this is the kiss of death. It's just that the "idea" of being put together—of someone else holding the strings, so to speak, seems to get on everyone's nerves.

One of the reasons groups like these are put together is to promote diversity. Every boy band, for example, has to have: a cute one, a rebellious one, a heartthrob, a suave, sophisticated one and a safe, could-be-your-best-friend-or-older-brother one. The qualities that make someone "cute" or "rebellious" are best noticed by a third party.

Another important element in pop music is this: if you're a pop singer, chances are you won't be writing any of your own songs. At least not for a long, long time. If you're in a pop group, it's likely that someone—the someone who put you together, probably—will choose producers and writers who will create songs for you. This is also not the worst thing in the world—they may be better at song writing than you are, after all. But singing songs you don't like or don't completely understand might stick in your craw.

Then there's the dancing. If you're going to be a pop performer, you gotta dance! Don't stress over it if you have two left feet—every boy (and girl) band has at least one member who's a little heavy on his or her feet. (Think about the boy and girl bands you know— you'll see we're right about that one.) You'll learn. Just break down the dance into individual moves and practice them over and over. Pretty soon, you'll be moving like Janet Jackson. Or a reasonable facsimile.

Finally, there are the costumes—yes, boy and girl bands usually wear costumes of some kind. Just be aware that what looks good on one group member will not necessarily look good on you, and plan accordingly.

## FOUR PHRASES EVERY POP GROUP SHOULD MEMORIZE!

1. "We want to take our music to the next level."
2. "We're edgier than other groups—we have more of an R&B/hip-hop/urban feel to our music."
3. "No one tells us what to say."
4. "We're not a boy/girl band."

## TYPES OF SONGS POP GROUPS CAN SING!

1. "We broke up and boy am I sad!" songs.
2. "We got back together and boy am I happy!" songs.
3. "We met and my life will never be the same!" songs.
4. "Boy, do we love our fans!" songs.

## SIGNS THAT YOU'RE IN A SUCCESSFUL POP GROUP!

1. There are at least three other groups that look and sound exactly like you.
2. People are asking for haircuts named after you.
3. Everywhere you go, you hear one of your songs playing the background (this includes at the local fast food restaurant and in airports.)
4. Fans see you on the street and scream uncontrollably.
5. Your untouched chicken salad sandwich is being sold for $3,000 on eBay.

## FOLK MUSIC . . . NO, YOU'RE NOT SERIOUS!

Once upon a time, there was an era called the '60s, and during the '60s, musicians believed that their music could make a difference and touch the world. They believed that music could heal strife, war, and general discontent. They were the folk singers. They sang songs that spoke to generations of alienated teenagers.

These days, very few people except for Alan M. keep the folk flame burning. First of all, listen to the radio—are there any stations that actually play folk music? No. Watch MTV (which you do anyway, 'cause you've got that thing for Carson Daly) and you'll see—no one is playing folk music! Even Jewel and Alanis, who are the closest things we have to folk singers have turned to other professions such as acting or writing until this singer/songwriter backlash is over.

But if you talk to Alan M., he'll tell you—folk music isn't about airplay or money or fame—it's about making music that matters, that touches the soul. And he might be right—after all, Josie is pretty crazy about his music, isn't she?

## ROCKIN' INTO TOWN!

OK, now back to being a rock star.

You've got your songs, you've got your look and you've got your band—now how do you get your music to the masses?

There are plenty of stories about record deals—no two bands got their deal the same way. And although Josie and the Pussycats were pretty lucky (talk about an overnight success!) most of the time, getting a record deal takes a long, long time.

Basically, you've got to get your music heard by the people who can do you the most good—those record company execs who drive big flashy cars and are always talking on cell phones. The best way to do that is to make a demo, which is basically a tape of you doing what you do best—singing and playing your instruments. Then you take that demo and mail it out to absolutely every record company you can think of, corporate and indie. Eventually, someone will give it a listen—and it will either be thrown out with yesterday's lunch, or it will land in the lap of someone who might be interested in making you a rock star.

Through it all, you must remember this mantra—do not be discouraged! Most rock stars do not become famous overnight—it takes years of work, sweat, and tears to get a record deal. Yes, we know . . . some people get record deals overnight, but they're the exception, so think positive and one day, your dreams will come true. If all else fails, you can put the record out yourself. CDs are fairly cheap to produce these days, and lots of people put out their own music. Look on the Internet and DIY!

## HOW TO KEEP IT TOGETHER!

Sometimes, bands break up. The Beatles broke up. And hey, if it can happen to the Beatles, it can happen to you.

So, what can you do to make sure your band never breaks up? You've got to try your hardest to get along with your bandmates!

Right now you're thinking, "Hey, these are my best friends! Of course we get along!"

Ahah! You say that now! But just imagine yourselves a few years down the road—when you're wildly successful and surrounded by fans, by fame, and by big burly bodyguards. The pressure of success has the power to break apart even the strongest friendships.

So what steps can you take to make sure you and your band are together, always and forever, like The Who?

*Give each other personal space! Yes, you're a rock band, but no, that doesn't mean you have to be joined at the hip. Make sure you make time for yourself.

*Give each other a break! Yeah, your drummer is a little zany, and your bass player is constantly beating up your manager and your manager is, well . . . let's just say a little off-the-wall. But remember, you've got some character flaws too—you just keep them hidden! Be good to your bandmates, and give them permission to be the people they are—don't try to change them into Mini-Me versions of you.

*Stay grounded! Success comes and goes, but friendship is forever—Josie and the Pussycats know that, and so should you! Remember where you came from and remember to stay humble—don't let the trappings of fame turn you into someone you're not.

*Stay true to yourself! So the record company wants you to do a cover album of Mariah Carey tunes—what's a rock band to do but crank up the volume on "Butterfly?" No, no, no—stay true and stand your ground, and let them know there are definitely some things you'll never, ever do!

*Take time to do non-band things together! Rehearsals, gigs, promotional tours, autograph signings, meet 'n greets—sometimes it seems like the bunch of you are always working, always talking about the music business, always reading the pop charts and watching MTV to see who's on top today (although you would definitely watch anyway, 'cause you've got that thing for Carson Daly). Make a date with your bandmates and spend the day doing the things you liked to do before you got famous—go shopping, hang out at the gym, go to the beach and surf or swim . . . you get the idea? Remember, friends first—keep that friendship fresh by making time for one another.

*Stay loyal in every way! If someone disses your drummer, stand up for her! If someone says your bass player is lame, open your mouth and let the critics know you won't stand for any trash talking about your bandmates—loyalty is key to keeping your band tight. And loyalty means no cheating on your buds: for example, let's say your lead singer/guitarist is dating a totally cool dude who sings sensitive, romantic love songs—and you suddenly realize that you've got a thing for him too! Don't ever, ever go for him— he's your best friend's guy, and that's that! Weird romantic entanglements are a sure-fire way to destroy a band!

*Remember—everyone is entitled to a bad day! So, your bass player's throwing a fit and your drummer has been missing for three days (check the closets, she may just be playing hide and seek!)—so what? Everyone is allowed to be moody now and then—you've probably had a few bad days yourself! So be patient and tolerant and remember—when you're feeling lousy, you'll be glad you have such thoughtful bandmates!

## "HOW TO" TIPS FROM JOSIE AND THE PUSSYCATS!

### JOSIE'S LOVE TIPS

You know Josie's in love with a totally great guy—Alan M. is handsome, talented, romantic, and totally impervious to insults about his name! But for Josie and Alan M., the path to true love was not without its bumps—and Josie remembers each and every crack! Here are some tips to make sure that your romance path is a little smoother!

*Be yourself! When Josie was crushing on Alan M., she wasn't always the smoothest cat in the litter box. She tripped on lamps, guitar cords, and even her own two feet whenever he was around—she was nervous and she wanted to impress him. Once Josie finally relaxed, she was able to deal with Alan M. as a friend—a friend that eventually became a partner in love!

*Show that special someone your skills! Alan M. may be able to write a beautiful love song, but he's clueless when it comes to fixing his truck. Enter Josie, who always knew her shop classes would come in handy! She's as talented with a wrench and a spark plug as she is with her guitar—she was always available to get Alan M.'s truck back in shape. And of course, she impressed him with her guitar playing and singing. The lesson? Don't be afraid to show your crush what you can do—and definitely don't pretend to be clueless or timid! Everyone likes a girl who can pump up the accelerator!

*Show Ms. or Mr. Right that you care! Too shy to come out and tell your crush how much you like her or him? You can show your fantasy date that you dig her or him in a thousand little ways! You can be supportive, you can be a friend, or you could even write a song for that person!

*Share with your crush! When Josie hit the

big time, she brought Alan M. along for the ride. (She would have been there to help him celebrate his big night, performing in a club, but of course she was dealing with subliminal messages and murderous management!). The point is, when something good happens to you, be sure to share the moment with your crush—let your crush enjoy it too. And when something major is going on with your hottie, be there to share the excitement.

*Don't be afraid of PDA! Hey, Josie and Alan M. shared their first smooch in front of thousands of screaming fans—how much more public can a display of affection be?

## VAL'S ANGER MANAGEMENT TECHNIQUES!

Valerie Brown is a cool, talented and very together young woman—until she gets angry. Then she pops a serious gasket—and takes down everything and everyone in her path. But she's working on it—everyday, she takes certain steps to help keep her temper under control. And it's working! Usually!

*Learn the power of meditation! "Good People Don't Get Angry..." or "My Fists Are Not My Friends" can be repeated over and over, like a mantra, until the stressful feeling passes.

*Talk about your problems! Spend time with friends who really care about you, and talk to them about your feelings—they probably have valuable ideas and can help you get through your tough times.

*Work it out! In times of stress, nothing feels better than a work-out. You can hit the gym and sweat out your tension by running on a treadmill or lifting some weights. Or take a high-kicking aerobics class and dance your troubles away.

*Hit things! A punching bag! A pillow! The ski slopes! Anything easily available will do. It's the only way to really get your aggressions out, after all!

## MELODY'S "STAY HAPPY" TIPS!

No matter what's happening around her, Melody always seems very happy . . . happy, happy, happy—that's Melody. Even when Carson Daly starts whacking her with cardboard Mariah Careys, Melody remains . . . happy. It's a skill.

*Surround yourself with friends! Melody knows that no matter what happens, she has her friends nearby. They're always available to show her love and support, and that makes her . . . happy.

*Surround yourself with animals! Animals make Melody very . . . happy.

*Surround yourself with sunshine! Melody is someone who knows the power of positive thinking—she can make lemonade with the absolutely sourest lemon. And thinking positive is definitely something that makes Melody very . . . happy.

## COULD YOU BE FRIENDS WITH A PUSSYCAT?
Take Our Test & Find Out!

Are you just like Josie? Very much like Val? Majorly like Melody? This quick quiz will let you know exactly which Pussycat you most resemble.

**1. You've got the day off and you're looking for something fun to do. What's the first thing on your list?**

a) Head out to the record store and check

out all the latest CDs.

b) Spend the afternoon at the gym, lifting weights and running on the treadmill.

c) Bounce over to the local pound and volunteer some time to work with the animals.

**2. You had a really bad day and you have to find a way to cheer yourself out of it. What do you do?**

a) Grab a pair of headphones and rock out to your favorite band.

b) Head over to the gym and punch a bag or jump some rope.

c) You never, ever have bad days.

**3. Your romantic soul mate is . . .**

a) Someone you can talk to and share secrets with; someone you have a lot in common with.

b) Someone who can keep up with you—someone active and energetic.

c) Someone cute, cuddly and sweet—like a human puppy dog.

**4. The most important quality in a friend is . . .**

a) Honesty & trustworthiness.

b) Loyalty

c) Sweetness & sincerity

**5. Your motto is ...**
a) Rock on, sister love!
b) If something is in your way, knock it over!
c) Honk If You Love Hugs & Rainbows!

**6. Your idea of the perfect evening with your friends is ...**
a) Popping popcorn, listening to music, and writing and sharing poetry.
b) Spending time doing something seriously hi-energy—bowling, smacking around some balls at a batting cage, or dancing up a storm at a club.
c) Doing each other's hair and nails, talking about your crushes.

**7. You're at the shopping mall-what's the first store you hit?**
a) Sam Goodys, Coconuts, or Record Town
b) Modells or Foot Locker
c) The pet store

**8. Your birthday is coming up-what's on your gift wish list?**
a) A new amplifier and some guitar strings.
b) A new amplifier and a punching bag—to replace the one you punched a hole in last month.
c) A new snare drum and a pet kitten.

**9. What quality do you share with a real live pussycat?**
   a) You're mysterious and you like spending time alone sometimes.
   b) You can jump phenomenal heights, and when someone steps on your tail, you scratch 'em.
   c) You're warm and cuddly.

**10. If you could only use one word to describe yourself, what word would it be?**
   a) Focused.
   b) Tough.
   c) Tender-hearted.

IF YOU ANSWERED . . .

. . . MOSTLY As: You and Josie are a match made in pussycat heaven.

. . . MOSTLY Bs: You and Val would be inseparable.

. . . MOSTLY Cs: You and Melody would be true blues forever.